Smiling, Nellie dreamed of flowers. They carried a sweet fragrance that seemed to be stronger than usual. Surrounded by them, the delicate petals tickled her nose, bringing her abruptly awake.

Her eyes opened in time to see a tawny, dark-haired stranger who squatted only inches away. Shifting aside, tiny twigs crunched under his weight. His eyes were brown, fringed with long black lashes.

The vision could have been a figment of her imagination. Dark-complexioned, he was likely of Indian descent. High cheekbones and a strongly carved nose gave his face a rakish appearance. His dark, untamed hair was in need of a cut.

How long had he been there? No wonder she had been dreaming of flowers. They were being held directly in her face!

A Time to Love

By Christy L. Hicks

June 6, 2004

*This first edition copy is
for Sandra Adams.*

Happy Reading!

Christy L. Hicks

Once Upon a Lifetime
Publisher

Scripture quotations taken from the
King James Version of the Bible

"We Shall Meet" by Robert P. Main
Standard Hymns and Spiritual Songs

Once Upon a Lifetime
Publisher
1381 Riley Farm Road
Axton, Virginia 24054

Library of Congress Control Number: 200309007
ISBN 0-9725035-0-1

Printed in the United States by Morris Publishing
3212 East Highway 30
Kearney, NE 68847
1-800-650-7888

Dedicated to my family- the people who made this book possible.

With special thanks to my sixth grade teacher, Mrs. Paula Collie- who helped with editing the work, and encouraged me to write when I was twelve!

Prologue

Eleanor peered down at the tiny wrinkles lining her pale hands. Sunlight falling through tall windows surrounding the fireplace could not hide the traces of time. Clutching the back of a chair for support, she gingerly reached for a small, hand carved pine box on the mantle.

From the box, she took out an old pewter frame holding a picture of a young, dark-haired soldier dressed in a gray Confederate uniform. Taken shortly after enlistment, the boy's features carried a hint of a smile. There were no shadows in his eyes then, for he had not yet witnessed the tragedies of war.

Burning in Eleanor's memory was another picture of her and the same youth standing where she stood now. It had been on a cold day with windblown snowdrifts outside the window. The fire had been warm and the boy had been laughing. Unfortunately, there was no frame to hold that moment.

Why, those days had been like a dream! Nearly sixty summers had come and gone. Pressing her nose against the windowpane, Eleanor gazed beyond the tree-lined valley and bright colored autumn leaves. Oblivious to her surroundings, she sighed... recalling another time.

1860
Chapter One

The Blue Ridge Mountains of Virginia rose behind Nellie as she entered the dark interior of the hen house. Despite the dim surroundings, she could see that it was going to be a clear, beautiful day. The sunrise peeked through the boarded walls, spreading tiny fingers across the straw. Breathing deeply, she inhaled the scent of loblolly pines that surrounded the Morgan farm. How she loved the fresh air of springtime!

Reaching beneath a hen, Nellie gathered three warm eggs. Hunger pains gnawed at her stomach, and she could almost taste the bacon and sunny-eyed eggs. She looked down, smiling. Someone else tasted them, too. The family's beagle followed along, sniffing at her heels. He watched as Nellie gathered the eggs, knowing that breakfast scraps was in the making.

Entering the breezeway between the cabin and kitchen, she found her mother placing thick slabs of pork in an iron skillet. The fragrant aroma of breakfast brought a smile to Nellie's face, while urging her brother and sisters from their beds. The smell of cooking was everyone's signal to wake-up.

"Here dear. Could you slice these?" Her mother held a bunch of spring onions by their long green shoots.

Soon the patter of small bare feet on the wooden floor competed with the sound of sizzling pork in the frying pan. Feeling a tug at her skirt, Nellie looked down to find her baby sister, Mary Ann, pleading to be held.

"Hold me," she insisted.

Kneeling down, Nellie gathered Mary's small form in her arms, kissing the little girl's rosy cheek. Mary's face carried an expression far beyond her three years. There was always a question lurking in her big blue eyes.

Careful to hold her baby sister away from the tear-causing onions, Nellie placed little Mary on the edge of her lap. She sat down near her brother John and two younger sisters, Rebecca and Laura.

The Morgans were a family of seven, and Nellie was the oldest child at fifteen. An onlooker would have found the brother and sisters very similar in appearance. From Scotch-Irish descent, their features were small, set inside oval faces, framed with reddish-blond hair. Small in stature, the children were sturdy despite their delicate frames.

Lightly freckled like the rest, Nellie was just beginning to lose her little girl features. Only recently had her cheekbones become more defined, making the dimple in her chin stand out. Despite her budding feminine figure, she continued to wear her hair in braids. The two plaits hung over her shoulders without ornament of ribbon or color.

Accustomed to the responsibilities of a first born, Nellie was out-spoken and independent. Having been told that her father had wanted a son, she had tried to make up for the loss. In fact, she much preferred the rugged outdoors to the confines of the cabin. Of course, her Pa had gotten his son. Her brother John had been born two years later.

Quickly chewing the salty pork, Nellie paid no attention to the taste in her mouth as she gulped a cup of water. When she had finished eating, she hopped lightly from her chair to place the empty plate in the wash pan.

There was a new horse in the barn that her father had recently acquired through a neighbor's trade, and the gelding was going to be hers. Finally, she was going to have her own horse!

Telling her parents that she was going to make friends with the animal, she was outside the door before her mother could warn her to be careful. Nellie was very quick on her feet, despite a slight frame that reached only five feet two in height. In a year, she would be sixteen, and still had not grown an inch since her thirteenth birthday. Although she had stopped growing in height, there were parts of Nellie that were continuing to sprout. Hiding these obvious signs of womanhood, she wore her mother's loose fit dresses.

Gathering a fistful of skirt, she adjusted the cloth so that her movements could not be hindered. Stepping up on the bottom wooden rail that kept the horses inside the barn, she flipped the braids over her shoulder. Nellie scrunched her nose when she detected the smell that belonged only to a horse. The gelding neighed. His gray coat blended well with the shadowed enclosure. Of considerable height and strength, he stomped his front hoof in defiance, throwing back his mane when Nellie stretched her hand cautiously forward.

Trying another tactic, Nellie swung a rope over the animal's neck. Shimmering at the unknown contact, it was a minute before the horse allowed himself to be lead into the morning sunlight. When Nellie reached up to stroke the smooth coat on the gelding's neck, only a slight protest was made. It wasn't long before the horse had stopped shifting, and Nellie managed to quickly place a blanket onto its back.

"Shhh. now. Everything's going to be okay. You be a good boy. I'm going to take care of you. I promise."

Relaxing in her presence, the horse appeared to sense the care in Nellie's whisper. The animal did not move when she turned aside to gather the harness and saddle that hung from a peg. Bending low, Nellie balanced the saddle on one shoulder. When she tried to transfer the bulky weight to the horse's back, she nearly fell from her perch on an overturned bucket. Puffing in frustration, she could see that both her legs and arms were entirely too short!

Dropping the heavy gear to the ground, she hurried impatiently back to the cabin. She reached the door just as her father was bringing in a pail of water from the spring. Her mother would be washing clothes today.

"Pa!" she called. "I'd like to try the new horse. Could you help me with the saddle?"

"Just wait for me in the barn," he answered.

She returned to the gelding that curiously arched his neck to sniff the air as Nellie approached. Well, she certainly hoped that she had passed inspection!

Holding his head at an angle, something caught his attention in the open doorway. Nellie turned in time to see her father coming forward, carrying a small pail. It was filled with russet colored, tangy crab apples.

"He'll like these," her father nodded towards the pail. With his free hand, he reached up to smooth the horse's coat.

"He's going to be your pet, Nell."

Her full name was Eleanor, and it was shortened to Nellie or Nell, depending on what was being said. Gesturing towards the fruit, he added, "You giving him the apples will be something like an Indian peace offering."

Nodding, Nellie placed an apple on her palm, holding it up to the horse. Sniffing the fruit, the gelding quickly opened his huge mouth. Nellie grimaced as she felt her entire palm being licked with a large, wet tongue. Ugh! She jerked her hand away when saliva dripped onto her wrist. The apple was devoured in seconds. Big brown eyes begged for more.

"He likes those. Looks like you're making a sure friend," her father chuckled.

To divert the gelding's attention from the saddle that was about to be thrown on, Nellie offered the remaining treats. The horse gave a small start when the weight settled on his back. Stepping nervously, he made it difficult for the bit to be placed in his mouth. He was broken-in but uneasy with strangers.

"Here," Joseph motioned for his daughter to stand back. "Why don't I try him out first? Get him used to being here."

"No," Nellie insisted kindly. "Please, Pa, I can handle him. He needs to know that I'll be the one in charge."

Joseph carefully handed the reins to his daughter.

11

"All right, but I'll be keeping close by. If you feel the least bit uneasy, don't go taking any wild hare chances, you hear."

Her father held the bridle while she quickly placed a foot in the stirrup and swung onto the saddle. The gelding's body jerked under the unexpected weight. Grabbing hold to the reins and to the animal's mane with both hands, she was prepared when the horse took off at a gallop.

"Hold on tight!" Joseph shouted. "He'll calm down. Just hold him close with your legs and don't let go of the reins!"

Much later, Nellie was managing the horse with little effort. It had taken nearly an entire afternoon to earn the animal's trust. Admiring the graceful lines under the mane that flowed as he galloped, Nellie decided to call the gelding, Breeze.

That night, Nellie went to bed with a smile. It had been a good day.

A few days later, she took Breeze into the woods where she spent most of her time. The familiar sound of the distant river encouraged Nellie to take the horse down to its edge for a taste. After the gelding had drunk his fill, he was tied to a nearby tree while Nellie sat down on a hollow log.

Peering at the ground, she examined a trail of ants crawling for shelter beneath the log. She had only been there for a short time when she saw a gray squirrel poke its head from behind the trunk of an oak tree. She watched the creature's unhurried skips as it scampered through the leaves in the direction of the river. Curious, she decided to follow the path it had taken.

Moving quietly on bare feet, she was careful to avoid any twigs or branches that would snap under pressure. When her father was a boy, his grandpa had taught him to tread softly. The habit had been handed down from the time her people had first come to this new land. At one time Indians had lived all over these parts and didn't trust the white man. To avoid trouble, the settlers had tried to keep out of their way.

But there had come a time when the settlers outnumbered

the Indians and they had chased the bronze people away. Pa had told them about the journey of the Cherokees that had taken place during the winter of '38 and '39. Much of the tribe had been marched to a territory out west while a few remained behind on a reservation in North Carolina.

Despite their absence, their legends lived on. A local story described an Indian girl and boy from different tribes who had fallen in love. When their parents had forbidden them to marry, they had climbed onto a big rock jutting above the huge Blue Ridge Mountain valley. Determined to be together one way or another, they had jumped.

Nellie shuddered. She had never seen the place, although she was told it wasn't far away. She imagined that their spirits still lingered near the cliff side known as Lovers Leap.

Sitting around late night campfires in the time of corn shucking and summer harvest, Nellie had often listened to the older men spin tales of adventure and near escape. At twelve, she had daydreams of walking through the wooded hills and meeting a tall, handsome warrior. It did not matter that they could not speak the same language. They communicated with gestures and smiles.

Lost in thought, she suddenly felt the ground disappear under her feet and looked down too late. With a splash and flailing arms, she reached to clasp the only substance within an arm's reach- water! Caught in her romantic musings, she had missed the wandering squirrel and found the river instead. Upon gaining footage, she was again taken by surprise.

The sight before her eyes could have been a scene from her daydreams. Oh, the river was spread out like a rippling silver blanket! But it was not the river that had caught her full attention. Someone was slipping quickly from the water, and making an exit through the trees. She caught a glimpse of a tan-muscled back that narrowed down to lean hips.

Nellie blinked. Was the retreating male a figment of her imagination? Her heart pounded. She grasped a root on the river's bank, pulling herself out of the water. Running to Breeze,

13

she wasted no time in urging the horse to a gallop. Branches tore at her dress and bare arms as they raced toward the safe haven of home.

At the sight of her family's cabin in the clearing, Nellie heaved a sigh of relief. She led Breeze to the small fenced area behind the barn and headed for shelter. The stranger was still in her thoughts when she sat down weakly. Her trembling legs threatened to buckle. Her sister Laura saw her staring at the knotted, boarded wall, and asked, "What's wrong, Nellie? Do you feel okay?"

At seven, Laura was a sensitive child. She could usually tell when something was not right. There were times when Nellie felt as though her sister was much older than seven, much older than her own fifteen years.

Laura's voice brought Nellie back to the present as she replied quietly, "Uh...I'm fine. I was just thinking that I should have been more careful when I was out riding."

Pulling her wet clothes away from her skin, she explained with a grimace, "You see, I wasn't looking where I was going and accidentally fell in the river."

Nellie's father heard this exchange, and his deeper voice traveled from another room as he walked towards them.

"Told you to be careful on that new horse. He's going to take some time of getting used to. You need to be paying attention from now on, you hear?"

Peering at his daughter, he continued, "You didn't run into any trouble today, did you Nell? I've told you to be careful when you go riding off by yourself. Not many girls your age spend the day in the woods. Most have got things on their mind like getting married and starting a family."

Nellie blocked out her father's words. She had heard this same speech many times before. Long ago she had decided that there was more to life than marriage and babies. But Joseph's tone of reproof reminded Nellie that she was getting older.

Afraid that he would tell her to stay indoors, she used her most convincing voice.

14

"Pa, everything's fine. I just had my mind on the farm and wasn't watching where I was going."

Her father cut in, "Well, since you have the farm on your mind, there's lots you can do. The weeds are taking over the garden. We'll have them pulled in no time with the two of us working. And your ma could use some help in the cabin. You've been getting off too easy with housework lately. It's time your ma taught you to be a lady."

Nellie felt a sinking sensation in her stomach. There were times when she didn't want to think about growing up.

Chapter Two

Forbidden to go beyond the field, the following week stretched out like a year. The usual rise and fall of the sun seemed to be taking its time overhead. Nellie tried to finish her chores early in the cabin so she could have the rest of the day for herself. She was anxious to get out into the woods.

When Joseph saw that his daughter was capable of performing a lady's work, he loosened his restrictions. One morning after she had helped her mother with the children, and was hanging freshly washed frocks out to dry, her father gestured towards the fields.

"Don't worry about the garden today, Nellie. We're caught up, and I know you're itching to get in the saddle." He laid his roughened, work-worn hand on her shoulder, nodding towards the barn. "Go on now. Just be careful, you hear?"

Nellie smiled gratefully. She rushed past her father, heading for the barn.

The sun was warm on her hair and face. She had no intention of returning for a while. Her bonnet was forgotten in the excitement of renewed freedom.

She tried not to rush through the motions of gearing Breeze, but she was eager to feel the wind in her hair. Placing a foot in the stirrup, she swung her body into the saddle, soon feeling the horse's movement. The gelding responded as though they were long-time friends. With the sun's heat on her back, she directed the horse towards the river.

The distance to the river seemed much shorter than usual. It took only seconds to secure Breeze to a poplar that grew near the river's edge. Pulling the cotton frock over her head and releasing the petticoat so that it fell to her feet, she stood in her cotton shift and bloomers. She glanced around anxiously, remembering the masculine form she had seen emerging from the water only a week before.

Shaking the thought aside, he must have been a figment of her imagination. Smiling, she stretched her arms high above her head. Why, she could almost touch the sky! At that moment she was the only person in the world. There was nothing but the river and an endless maze of trees. Rivers in the mountains were clear and deep. What appeared to be shallow water of only a few inches was actually chest level further out.

Dipping her toes into the swirling water, Nellie was pleased to feel the day's heat slowly ease away. Adjusting to the water's cool temperature, she waded farther out. It was not long before the water was nearly touching her waist, and she lay on her back to float. Spreading her arms, she felt the current billow beneath the thin, cotton shift.

Watching the clouds above, she soon knew that she had drifted a good ways when the tree branches nearly obscured the sky. She rose up in time to see a water snake slide into the depths from the opposite shore. It was time to get out. Rather than feel alarmed at the reptile's presence, she knew that the snake was probably more frightened of her. Still, she didn't care to share the river.

Swimming quickly back up stream, she silently thanked her father for teaching her to swim. She had seen the river swell after a mighty rainstorm and knew that the rising water could pose a threat. Just last summer the river had risen and uprooted a tall, poplar tree in its path. Looking up now, she saw the tree spanning the riverbed. It made a nice footbridge.

Rising out of the water, she pulled the clinging cotton dress away from her frame. Shaking the wet cloth lightly, she hoped that the wind would fan it dry. Frowning, she did not welcome the thought of making contact with Breeze's hairy coat. Plucking a hundred hairs from her damp clothing didn't appeal in the least.

Collecting her frock and petticoat from the ground, she tossed them over the horse's back. Taking hold of the gelding's reins, she led him to a crooked crab apple tree not far from the river's bank. The tree had been burdened down with fruit that now lay ripened around its base.

Unbraiding her hair, Nellie used four fingers to comb through the heavy, wet strands. Fanning the dampened locks with her hand, the tresses fell over her shoulders in disarray.

Stooping, Nellie picked some tiny lavender flowers growing beneath the shade of laurel. She held them up, inhaling their simple fragrance. With the blooms nestled between her thumb and forefinger, she sat down to allow the sun's rays to dry her hair and frock.

Propping her back against the rough bark of a neighboring oak, she rested her eyes, tired from the water and the warm summer sun. Soothing, the shade eased her mind, and she soon fell into a light sleep, the wild flowers falling from her fingers.

Smiling, Nellie dreamed of flowers. They carried a sweet fragrance that seemed to be stronger than usual. Surrounded by them, the delicate petals tickled her nose, bringing her abruptly awake.

Her eyes opened in time to see a tawny, dark-haired stranger who squatted only inches away. Shifting aside, tiny twigs crunched under his weight. His eyes were brown, fringed with long black lashes. Her heart jumped. She sat fully upright, jarring the flowers that were being held beneath her nose. Her mind screamed, while fear lodged in her throat. A hot flush burned her cheeks. Shielding the damp shift with crossed arms, she scrambled back, feeling the tree's rough bark scratching her skin.

Surely she must be dreaming! Dark-complexioned, he was likely of Indian descent. High cheekbones and a strongly carved nose gave his face a rakish appearance. His dark, untamed hair was in need of a cut.

The stranger's presence was unnerving. How long had he been there? No wonder she had been dreaming of flowers. They were being held directly in her face!

Suddenly, and ever so gently, he smiled. Why, he could only have been about twenty. Playfully, he reached forward, brushing the petals across her cheek.

Nellie jerked away, warding off the touch.

"Leave me alone!" she demanded. Despite her attempted self-confidence, she could not disguise the tremor in her voice.

Quickly, the stranger dropped the flowers.

"Hey, I wasn't going to hurt you."

Nellie averted her eyes.

He settled back on his heels as if sensing her discomfort.

"I'm Jacob Hunter, by the way. People call me Jake. Pleased to meet you, Miss- ?" His casual question hung in the air.

"Nellie Morgan," she said with a sniff.

"Hmm. A right common name for someone who lives under the trees." A grin tugged at the corners of his lips.

Nellie fastened her eyes on the tan column of his throat wondering if he was the one who lived somewhere in the trees. He certainly looked as if he were cut out to live among them. Rationally, she did not give voice to her thoughts.

"Our cabin is close by," she replied. Nellie sensed the interest that crossed his features. She quickly added, "I was just out riding and should be heading back."

He peered at Nellie.

"You telling the truth? Because I haven't seen any houses nearby." Not waiting for a response, he continued, "You really should be more careful out here alone."

Before he could say another word, she interrupted. "I can take care of myself. My pa taught me good."

She knew she had answered too quickly when his face suddenly descended close to hers. Before she could turn her head, his mouth grazed her lips.

19

"I should hope so," he murmured.

When he pulled his mouth away, Nellie's cheeks burned with embarrassment. She glanced up to find his brown eyes crinkling with amusement. While the kiss had meant to reinforce a point, it left her both shaken and breathless. She felt annoyed at his silent *I told you so* look.

The stranger stood up and gazed at some distant focal point that Nellie could not discern. With his back to her, Nellie seized the opportunity for flight. Running, she somehow managed to loosen Breeze's tether from the tree while swinging into the saddle. Spurring the horse to a gallop, she clutched her frock, petticoat and reigns with a tight fist. Risking a glance over her shoulder, she saw that he was still standing in the same spot. He hadn't made a move to follow her.

That night, after supper had been eaten, Nellie lay snuggled against her sisters in the upstairs loft. Her thoughts returned to the stranger she had met earlier in the day. Relieved, she had managed to escape in the nick of time.

Riding through the woods in her bloomers, she must have been a sight. Expelling a deep breath, Nellie had been mortified! Stopping at the outer edge of the field, she had quickly donned her clothes before reaching the cabin. Fortunately, there were no questions from her family, and she had kept busy to avoid suspicion.

Picturing the stranger, she had difficulty in calling him boy or man. He was clearly older than her fifteen years. A boy really didn't become a man until he had a wife and family. Perhaps he did have a family, she thought.

Puzzled, she wondered why he had changed roles on her. One moment he had been charmingly harmless, and then she had been caught off-guard with his unexpected kiss. How dare he think he could invade her privacy, especially when she was trying to fall asleep!

Closing her eyes, Nellie hoped she'd never lay eyes on Jake Hunter again.

Chapter Three

Heavy drops of rain pounding on the tin roof awoke Nellie the following morning. The darkened sky seemed to reflect the gloom she had felt in her sleep. Frowning, she was unable to remember the dream. She had been searching for something that was inches within her grasp. Only everything was obscured by darkness.

Breathing on the misty windowpane, she could see that the downpour was creating growing puddles in the yard below. For once, she was happy to be indoors. She stared at the field lined with trees, imagining that she could see beyond the heavy branches. The ground, covered with pine needles and leaves, would be soggy. It would be impossible for her feet to remain dry when she stepped outside.

Where was the stranger? Was he sheltered? Wet? Cold? He had irritated Nellie, but she found herself feeling sorry for him. Actually, she would pity anyone left out in this weather. Determined not to dwell on his plight, she reached for a warm calico frock. The dress would afford protection against the damp outdoors.

She hurried out to gather the eggs, holding a cloth above her head. Breeze moved restlessly under the overhanging shelter at Nellie's approaching steps. Nudging his nose towards Nellie's hand, the gelding offered a greeting.

The barn door swung open again as her brother, John, came dripping through. His wet hair confirmed that he must have taken extra time to feed the ducks. At thirteen, her brother was a tall, thin, quiet boy who spent much of his time caring for the farm animals. He was a favorite with the baby chicks who would flock to his outstretched palm, knowing he held a meal of corn kernels.

Making a dash for the cabin, Nellie was ready to prepare breakfast. Absentminded, she rounded sausage patties that were flattened against an iron skillet. The sizzle and aroma of smoked pork soon filled the room, and soft creaks alerted her that she was no longer alone.

Nellie's mother, Martha, stepped to her daughter's side. Holding a shawl around her shoulders, she used her free arm to give Nellie a hug.

"Good morning, dear. I would have been up sooner had the rain not kept me awake most of the night. You didn't have to start breakfast without me," she said in an apologetic tone.

"That's okay, Ma. I woke up early and couldn't go back to sleep."

After the first pan of sausage had been cooked, Nellie replaced it with another while her mother prepared a boiling kettle of coffee. The aroma brought her father into the room, for he always enjoyed a cup to start his day. Nellie's sisters, one at a time, began to pad down the ladder in their stocking feet.

It was still raining after breakfast so Nellie climbed back up to the loft to finish a project she had started during the past winter. Folding the patchwork quilt across her bed, she went to the wardrobe that her father had built against the far wall.

From the top drawer, she took out a pair of soft doeskin moccasins. Near the moccasins was a worn leather drawstring pouch filled with brightly colored beads. They had belonged to her great-grandmother Sarah.

Nellie smiled gently, remembering the aged, soft-spoken lady who had come to live with them when she was eighty-some years old. This had been her father's grandmother who had outlived her sons and daughters.

Rain pattered on the roof and Nellie could hear her

grandmother's voice again, almost as if it were yesterday. With a far away look in her eyes, Grandma Sarah had forgotten the little girl at her feet, and Nellie had learned a well-kept secret. Her grandmother's first love had been a Cherokee Indian. Grandma Sarah had never told anyone about meeting Cloud Walker. They had met one day in the woods when she was gathering herbs. She had fallen down, hurting her ankle. The brave had come along, finding her sprawled on the ground. Helping her up, he had introduced himself with signs and words she didn't understand. And Grandma had known at that moment that she had fallen in love.

"Just like that," she had said, snapping her fingers.

They had been meeting for three months when one day he had explained that he must go far away. He had begged her to come with him, but she knew that she could not. Reluctantly, he had left. He had given her the pouch of keepsake beads and suggested that she sew them on dress fronts, above her heart. In this way he would always be close.

Grandma Sarah had spoken often of Cloud Walker in her last days, but had made no mention of the beads.

At her death, Nellie's mother had been very surprised to find a small leather pouch tucked inside Grandma Sarah's bodice, but Nellie had understood. Grandma was keeping Cloud Walker close to her heart as she journeyed from this life to the one awaiting them both. The gift was a token of love that time had not erased.

Cupping her palm, Nellie felt the beads' cool surface pour into her hand. She counted out a small quantity- twenty-five for each moccasin. Nearly a handful remained, and she placed them back into the pouch

She fingered the soft leather, closing her eyes to visualize the young brave who had touched the very same pouch. The image that came immediately to her mind was that of the strikingly attractive Jake Hunter. Smiling, she held the pouch tightly, pretending that she had been the one presented the token of love. Abruptly, she dismissed the thought.

Working carefully, she threaded the beads to form two intertwining circles that would be sewn above the moccasin's toes. The circles symbolized the bonding of two people, and the person who wore them would carry her with him wherever he roamed. Absorbed in her task, she had not noticed the passing morning until her stomach rumbled loudly. It was time to eat.

Her mother's summons provided a break in her thoughts.

"Nellie, could you please give me a hand with supper? The little ones are getting hungry."

"I'll be right down," she called.

Martha looked pleasantly surprised when she saw the moccasins cradled in her daughter's hands. She was puzzled as she admired Nellie's handiwork.

"Those look really comfortable. Where did you find the pretty beads?"

Before Nellie could answer, recognition dawned. "Why, those are the beads that belonged to your grandmother Sarah, aren't they?"

"Yeah. I wasn't going to use them just yet, but they look like they were meant for these moccasins. Of course, I still have a handful left."

Martha took the shoes from her daughter's hands, and held them at an angle beneath the light. She spoke more to herself than to Nellie when she commented, "Yes, I think they belong there, too."

Later, at the table, the Morgans bowed their heads, linking their hands as Joseph gave thanks for their food.

"Dear Lord, we ask that you bless this meal. Thank you for watering the garden today, and please watch over us and keep us throughout the day."

"Amen," was chorused by the entire family.

Conversation between bites of food concerned the upcoming harvest. The vegetables were beginning to ripen, and her father worried that he couldn't manage the crops alone. He'd probably have to ask their closest neighbor, George, for help this season. In exchange, he'd offer a small share of the crop.

On the following morning, Nellie quickly made her way to the fields, eager to put the day behind her. Despite the wet dirt clinging to her bare toes, she was glad the storm had broken the rising heat. It had rained during the night, and moisture hung in the air. Inhaling the freshness, she watched the ground as she walked, careful to sidestep the rambling vegetation.

Finding a hoe propped against the trunk of a tree, she joined her pa and brother in unearthing the potatoes that were beginning to peep through the ground. A pattern developed as the hoe rose and fell, nudging and pulling potatoes loose from their roots. They would have a cellar full this year.

At mid-day when the sun's heat became nearly unbearable, they stopped to rest in the shade. Her father was sprawled on the grass, breathing more heavily than usual.

"You all right, Pa?"

He mumbled something that she couldn't hear clearly. His voice was muffled in the arm that rested over his face. She was about to ask again, when her mother came forward with a cool jug of spring water.

"Joseph, are you feeling okay?" Martha asked.

Before answering, he took a huge gulp of the refreshing liquid, wiping his face on the sleeve of his arm.

"Yeah, I'm all right. Can't let this heat get the best of me."

She sat down beside him, using her hand to fan his reddened face.

"Why don't you come inside to rest? You have done enough for one day."

Nellie was surprised when her father didn't protest. Normally, he would have argued that he was fine, and continued working 'til dusk. Instead, he lay down after leaving the fields. Nellie heard her mother humming softly as she soothed his tight muscles with the gentle pressure of her fingers.

Hours spent tending to the crop over the next few days were shortened when her father decided to take his wife's

25

suggestion. He rested three full days before returning to the field.

On the morning that her father was due to get back to work, Nellie was reluctant to get out of bed. Spoiled, she was getting accustomed to sleeping the few extra hours. She and John had both been allowed to take a break from their work, although they had continued laboring a few hours a day.

Gently easing away from her sisters, Nellie yawned. She took extra time getting out of bed, dressing in an unhurried fashion. Knowing that she was probably taking too long, Nellie gradually made her way slowly outdoors.

Across a field of leafy vegetation, two figures stooped at intervals, dropping potatoes into a bushel basket. She rubbed her eyes against the bright glare of the morning sun. Squinting, she could not recognize the two men. Relieved, she was happy to find that the day's work would not be so tiring. Neighboring help was always welcome. Nellie was thankful that her father had followed through with his earlier plan.

"Nell!" her father called.

She turned around in surprise to find that her father was not in the field. His voice came from the barn behind her. Peering back at the field, she recognized the wiry figure of their neighbor, George as he straightened from his labors. Before she could identify the second person, her father spoke again, this time much closer.

"Didn't you hear me calling?"

She turned at the sound of his voice, a question marking her expression. Joseph gestured towards the two figures in the fields.

"George and his friend are helping me out today. My back's giving me the death of a time," he remarked, rubbing his spine.

"Always thought I could do anything, but seems this here is the good Lord's way of trying to tell me something. Ain't as young as I used to be and that boy out there helping George is strong as a whip," he finished with a gesture towards the field.

Looking at her father's face, Nellie noticed the lines etching his brow. Crows' feet touched the corners of his eyes as he squinted against the morning sunlight. Signs of laughter were evident in the creases that ran from his nose to the outer corners of his mouth. In a face stained reddish-brown by the sun's heat, he suddenly looked much older than his 47 years. Gazing at her father intently, she couldn't remember a time when he had looked any different.

Pondering the quick passage of time, Nellie realized that she, too, had aged during the last few years. While wrinkles had not yet mapped her face, a greater awareness of time had registered when her grandmother Sarah had died. What did the Bible say about life? That it was a vapor that appeared for a little while, and then vanished away.

Glancing down at her unlined hands, Nellie wondered how she would look in forty years. Where would she be? Would she marry? She peered at George now. In his late forties, the man had never married. Sometimes she wondered if he liked living alone.

She and her father walked toward the men in the field. Advancing closer, Nellie caught her breath. The unknown face, sheltered beneath the brim of the hat, looked oddly familiar. Straightening to full height, the stranger tipped his hat in greeting.

"Jake, I'd like you to meet my daughter, Nellie." Joseph nudged her near with a prod from his elbow.

"Hello, ma'am." Jake spoke quietly, as though meeting her for the first time. A serious expression had replaced the laughing eyes that had teased her in the woods.

"Pleasure to meet you," he said huskily, offering his hand.

Cordially, she nodded her head in greeting, avoiding his out-stretched arm.

Her father spoke, unaware of the friction, "Nell will be working in the field with us. If you need a helping hand with anything, just give her a call."

Studying the ground, Nellie was unprepared when Joseph announced that Jake would be staying in the barn since George's place wasn't set up for two people.

She took the hoe from her father numbly, as he walked back to the barn. Uncomfortable, Nellie felt Jake's eyes warming her shoulder blades. Determined not to acknowledge their prior meeting, she grasped the hoe, moving several rows away. Giving him a brief look as she stepped aside, she was annoyed to find bold mischief dancing in his eyes.

"So, we meet again, huh?" he murmured with a disarming smile. Nellie flinched, straightening her back.

Turning to him again, she whispered beneath her voice, "If my pa ever found out that you..." she broke off, not wanting to finish the sentence. Remembering the kiss in the woods brought a blush to her cheeks.

"...he would be very angry," she continued. "I don't want any trouble. So you keep out of my way, and I'll keep out of yours."

Resuming his work, the stranger said distantly, "No problem."

A silent rift continued to separate them throughout the day. Nellie couldn't decide whether she should be pleased or annoyed.

At noon, when they were sitting beneath the shaded maple, her father and George carried the conversation. Jake only spoke when addressed. Quieter than usual, Nellie could not bring herself to join in. She feared that talk could possibly force her to speak to Jake against her will.

Later, back in the field, Nellie's eyes strayed to his bent torso. She couldn't resist admiring the muscles that rippled beneath his shirt. How could she remain hostile with this attractive stranger?

At supper, Jake was asked to join the family. Nellie felt uncomfortable sitting across from him at their small wooden table. She felt his warm knees gently brush hers as they sat facing one another. Nellie found her food difficult to swallow, and was aware only of their guest's powerful presence.

She watched Jake's face as the lantern's soft, warm light threw patterns across it. In shadow, he appeared boyish, and Nellie wondered how much longer she could go on with her silence. She was surprised to see his eyes grow tender when young Rebecca told him about the little rabbit that she and Laura had seen that morning. Watching his expression, she was reminded of a father listening to a child. Was it possible that he wasn't quite as bad as she believed?

Chapter Four

Two weeks had passed, and despite an earlier determination to avoid Jake, Nellie had gradually let down her defenses. Working in the field had thrown them onto common ground. Some tasks required two people, and somehow she and Jake had been thrown helplessly together in a working relationship. For instance, carrying a bushel basket from the fields was made a lot easier when two people carried the load on opposite sides.

Allowing her tired muscles to relax, Nellie sat, leaning back against the porch banister. She dangled her legs over the edge, rocking gently. The night air was filled with the steady hum of crickets, while a whippoorwill's call sounded far away. It was late Saturday night and the family was gathered on the porch. There would be no getting up early the next day because there was no work on the Sabbath.

Her father was describing a scolding he had gotten as a boy. He and his mother had been visiting his Aunt Wilmoth. While the two sisters were busy talking, he had wandered off and found a tin of cookies. Curious, he had taken off the lid, and the tin had turned, spilling treats all over the floor.

"Yeah, I was a mite small, but it didn't matter. My ma said she'd whip me good if she ever caught me snooping again. Tell you the truth, I thought Aunt Wilmoth didn't mind me eating her sweets." Everyone chuckled.

Jake sat beside Nellie on the porch steps, and she felt his

shoulders tremble slightly as he laughed. He was adjusting well to their family life. In fact, if a stranger were to walk by, he'd never think that Jake was an outsider. Of course, he didn't look like the Morgans; his dark features contrasted greatly with their fair blond hair and blue eyes. But still, he fit in. Her parents treated him like a son and encouraged him to feel at home.

The night was clear, and cooler temperatures had replaced the day's warmth. A full moon cast splays of ghostly shadows on nearby trees and bushes. Rising from the porch, Nellie walked towards the field. She sometimes enjoyed being alone before joining her sisters in bed.

The voices of her family were a soft murmur when she sat on the dew-moistened ground near the barn. Lifting an arm above her head, she felt almost as if her fingers could touch the heavens. She wondered if the thought of touching the sky had ever entered anyone's mind.

Peering at the night sky, she found it easy to imagine a place where there was no darkness or sleep. While the earth had sunlight only for daytime, the heavens had a thousand lights.

Hugging knees to her chest, Nellie rested her cheek against folded arms. It was almost as though she was the only person in the world at that moment. But she wasn't. Movement near the trees caught her eyes. A tall silhouette was walking into the woods. It was Jake. Where was he going at this time of night? Nellie felt drawn to follow him. She'd tread quietly, and he would never know that she was near.

Cautious, she kept a safe distance. She cleverly stopped every few paces to listen for his footfalls. Should she keep following him? He was going deeper into the forest. Worried, Nellie knew she should turn back. Hadn't he once warned her about being out alone?

Standing still, she strained her ears in the silence. Unfortunately, she heard nothing but her quickened breathing.

"Would you mind telling me why you're following me?" The husky male voice was only an arm's reach away.

Startled, Nellie jumped.

Her heart racing, she couldn't speak. What would she tell him? That she was nosy?

"You really should be more careful. Your parents like me, but I don't think they'd want you out here with me at this time of night."

She sensed a smile on his face, although she could not see it.

"Is there any particular reason why they'd consider you a threat?" she taunted.

"Now, wait a minute little girl. Who's asking *who* the questions?"

He chuckled softly, turning in the direction they'd come. "Come on, we'd better start heading back before your pa comes after me with a shotgun."

Nellie walked along silently, feeling as though she had been dismissed.

"You want to answer my question?" he stated bluntly.

Breathing deeply, she decided to tell the truth. "I was curious. So I decided to follow, that's all."

"Well, now that your curiosity has been satisfied, what do you think?"

"That you like to take walks in the dark for no reason at all."

Grinning, he spoke, "Oh yeah. And what could I say about you?" He paused. "That you like to follow men around in the dark." He chuckled again. "Well, it looks like we have something in common."

Nellie had to smile.

"Let's just say that I'm glad you finally made a move to get acquainted, even if it did take a walk in the dark. We've been working together for what, two weeks? And you've been avoiding me like the plague."

What did he expect, she thought. As they walked along, Nellie felt the barrier between them slowly disappear.

"Yeah, I guess it is about time we put everything behind us. You've been pretty good these past couple of weeks." she said.

He stopped, and stretched out his hand. They shook.

Feeling more comfortable, she felt compelled to ask him the question that had been lurking in her thoughts.

"What brought you to work for my pa?"

He must have been expecting this question, for he replied, "I've been by myself for some time, and I just got tired of wandering around, with no place to go, and no place to call home." He paused, and continued, "Well, I knew you lived close by, so one day I found you and your pa working in the fields. I could see your pa needed help, and I'll admit, I was a bit curious about you." He sighed as he apologized, "I'm really sorry for the way I acted the day I found you asleep in the woods. You looked very pretty, and I just acted on impulse."

Jake thought she was pretty! The compliment brought a warm glow to her cheeks.

He looked away from her and she knew that he wasn't accustomed to making apologies.

"That's okay," she said with a smile. "An impulse sounds a lot like a girl I know who follows men around in the dark."

He laughed softly.

"I just hope Ma and Pa are asleep," she said in a worried voice as they came into the field. She heaved a sigh of relief, for there was no light burning in the cabin when they walked into the clearing. Her parents probably thought that she had already come in. With the little ones underfoot, she would not have been missed. Careful not to awaken anyone, Nellie opened the door only a crack. She had never been so happy to hear her father's snoring!

Peering down at Nellie with dancing eyes, Jake spoke in a deep, father-like tone, "A girl your age has no business running around this late at night. Now get inside before some wild man comes along and carries you away."

Catching her smile, Jake breathed a sigh.

"Seriously though, Nellie. I've never been more thankful to hear a man's snoring in all of my life." With that, he ruffled her hair, and said goodnight.

Despite getting in so late that night, Nellie awoke the next morning early as usual. It was the Sabbath. Her sisters had gotten up earlier, and were getting dressed. A beam of sunlight fell across the floor bathing her in its path. She pulled a faded calico dress over her head.

There was no church nearby, so the Morgan's spent their Sunday mornings in a worship service at home. Following breakfast, her father read Bible scriptures where Jesus had been tempted by the devil. Nellie listened intently, aware that her feelings for Jake bordered on a temptation of sorts. While her circumstances were different, she felt guilty for admiring him in a very unfriendly-like fashion. His attractive, dark looks were not going unnoticed. Well, it was no wonder since they worked side-by-side every day.

Reluctantly, she turned her focus to the hymn that her mother was now leading. It was an uplifting song about loved ones meeting again in heaven.

We shall meet beyond the river, by and by;
And the darkness will be over, by and by;
There our tears shall all cease flowing, by and by;
All the blest ones, who have gone
To the land of life and song-
We shall meet beyond the river, by and by.

Closing her eyes, Nellie tried to imagine that day. She would see Grandma Sarah again, and there would be other people that she had never met. Her mother's parents, for instance. Would they recognize her? Yes, she favored the family.

She peered at Jake. Would he be there, too? Jake sat quietly during these family gatherings, and Nellie wondered if his family had gone to church. Surely they did. Everybody worshipped the Lord.

After prayer, Nellie deeply inhaled the scent of morning air when she walked outdoors. The fragrance of overturned earth mingled with the sharp smell of pine sap. The buzzing hum of locusts promised another hot August day.

She headed for the paddock to find Breeze. It was going to be a beautiful morning for riding. Movement caught her eye, and she saw Jake leading Breeze from the barn.

"Good morning. I thought you'd be coming out for a ride, so I've geared your horse." Chuckling, he rubbed the gelding's neck affectionately.

"She wasn't too friendly until I lured her with a taste of honey."

"Would you like to come with me?" Nellie asked. The words had left her mouth before she could think. She hoped that he wouldn't refuse.

"Sure. I'll take the black horse."

This surprised Nellie. Her father had gotten the stallion about the same time that he had bought Breeze. No one had taken the opportunity to fully train him since much of the time was spent in the garden.

Jake looked at Nellie with raised eyebrows.

"Your pa said if I could stay on his back, I could use him while I'm here." He paused and grinned. "But if the thought of me falling worries you, we can share your horse."

"Oh no, " she countered quickly, glancing away. "It isn't that I don't think you can handle the horse. It's just that he hasn't really been ridden a lot."

Jake grinned down at her with that old mischievous glint in his eyes and assured Nellie that everything would be okay. Instantly, she pictured Jake coaxing the big horse with a hand greased in honey, crooning to him in a persuasive voice. She laughed.

Jake was puzzled by her sudden laughter, but he soon joined in when she explained the picture in her mind. When their chuckles subsided, he told her that he had become acquainted with the stallion. At night, he often visited the horse, and had gradually encouraged the animal to eat from his fingers. She had to admit, the animal certainly didn't appear skittish in his

35

company.

Deciding to ride bareback with only a blanket for comfort, Nellie mounted Breeze. She had only managed to throw one leg over the horse's back when she felt Jake's hand under her foot. Not expecting his help, she did not have time to pull the calico dress modestly over her legs. The fabric stretched above her thighs, and she flushed in embarrassment. She quickly rearranged her skirt, hoping that he hadn't noticed her color.

Distracted, she fumbled for the reigns as Jake mounted the stallion. The other horse was much taller than Breeze. Anxiously, she saw that he wasn't going to use a saddle. She hoped that he would be safe. Seeing the question register in her eyes, Jake remarked, "This may come as a surprise to you, Nellie, but I do know horses. My uncle taught me to ride before I could walk." He grinned.

"Oh," she murmured, feeling silly. He obviously knew a lot more about horses than she did.

As they passed her brother, she told John to tell their father that she and Jake were taking the horses out for exercise. They rode at a slow, steady pace, and there seemed no need for words. The river drew them, although it had not been a planned destination. Actually, they had not spoken of where they would go. It was almost as though the horses had led the way. Of course, Breeze was very accustomed to being led to the river. It seemed only natural that he should follow the pattern today.

Both horses picked up their gait when the water came in sight. The dry, summer heat had intensified their thirst. While the animals were refreshing themselves, Nellie heard a rustle. She turned her head to glimpse a small salt and pepper colored squirrel darting up a tree. She wondered if it was the same one whose path had led her to Jake.... or had the creature led him to her? Probably so. Its appearance was like an omen. The squirrel had been the reason that she was drawn to the area when she had first met Jake. It was hard to believe that so much had happened as a result of that day.

She and Jake cupped their hands together, drinking along

with the horses. This time when Jake placed a palm under her foot for support, she murmured, "Thank you."

"Is there any place you'd care to go?"

"Oh, it really doesn't matter," answered Nellie. "You choose."

Jake turned his horse, whom he called Storm, upstream.

"Okay. Let's go."

She practically had to spur the gelding to keep up with his lead. They had been riding for about fifteen minutes when they approached a large weeping willow. As if planned, Jake dismounted the stallion, and Nellie did the same.

Brushing the willows aside, Jake gestured toward the entrance with an outstretched arm. Inside the shaded canopy, the scene looked like something from a mystical world. Nellie could imagine fairies hovering above her, their small wings fanning the air. Soft, green moss lay over the ground like a carpet, with small purple forget-me-nots creating a flowered pattern.

After she sank down to her knees on the soft carpet, Jake said, "Just a minute," and disappeared.

Nellie wondered where he had gone. She became worried when he did not return right away. When nearly five minutes had passed, the branches parted. Jake had returned, and he was not empty-handed. In his open palms, he held more than a handful of black berries.

When her mouth opened in surprise, Jake took the opportunity to place a tangy berry on the tip of her tongue. She closed her mouth, timidly biting into the fruit.

"Is it good?"

She nodded.

"That was sweet of you," she murmured. "Thanks."

They finished the berries in silence, and Nellie was beginning to feel uncomfortable.

"How did you find this place? I don't think I've ever seen it."

"Well, I happened to come onto it when I was looking for a place to rest."

"Oh," she said.

Propping his back against the tree, he stretched out his legs, crossing them at the ankles.

"Before I started working with your pa, I didn't have a place to stay." He gazed out at a point in the branches as he spoke. Focusing on a scene that was invisible to Nellie's eyes, he recounted the story of his past. In half an hour, Jake skimmed over his life. Nellie learned that his parents had died when he was an infant. He didn't remember them, and had been raised by his grandmother. An only child, there were no sisters or brothers. He spoke of his grandmother's failing health, preceding her death two years before. Not wishing to be a burden on his relatives, he had struck out on his own. There had been no destination in mind. He had wandered from place to place, often living off of the land. He had thought to settle down in eastern Tennessee where he had worked for a blacksmith the previous winter. Restless, he had left when spring arrived, and made his way towards the Blue Ridge Mountains of Virginia.

By the time Jake finished his story, he had matted the moss beneath his feet where he paced back and forth. Stretching his arms above his head, he sighed. Reaching down, he grasped Nellie's hands, pulling her upright. Catching her breath, she wasn't prepared for the close contact with his broad chest. She felt awkward, yet could not look away from the muscles outlined tautly beneath his shirt. When he spoke, the movement in his throat caused his sun-bronzed skin to flex.

"Nellie," he said huskily, "As much as I'd like to, we can't be staying here all day."

He tugged her gently, adding, "Let's get going."

For the most part, Nellie remained quiet on their return journey. She hoped that he hadn't noticed her attraction to him. She felt at peace with their blossoming friendship, although she questioned her growing feelings for him.

In the following days, Nellie and Jake spent much of their time talking as they worked. Oddly, he seemed to treat their relationship like that of a brother and sister. Her parents didn't seem to mind their closeness and looked upon Jake as an addition to the family. Although he had taken up residence in the barn, his meals and time were shared with the Morgans.

He had been with them for almost two months when Joseph suggested a small room be built onto the cabin. The added room would provide extra living space for the family as well. John had been making a pallet on the family room floor, and would now be able to share a room with Jake. With winter coming up, it would be too cold to stay in the barn. Jake thanked her father, and Nellie felt somewhat nervous at the prospect of Jake living within such close quarters.

Chapter Five

The wind whipped Nellie's hair in her eyes as large drops of rain fell from the sky. Water ran in tiny streams down her face, causing her to stumble. She could vaguely see Jake's form running about fifteen feet ahead. The forest appeared to have swallowed all but the narrow strip of road on which they were traveling. Drenched, she trudged on blindly.

They had been visiting the new mill in Dan's meadow to buy cornmeal. Nellie had never seen anything like it! The scene could have been painted on canvas. On the outside, the mill appeared quite tranquil, perched on a pond and sitting against a backdrop of autumn colors. A large wooden wheel turned against the side of the building, moved by the pressure of water channeled in from a nearby stream.

Upon getting closer, the peace had been broken by the hum of activity as two large stones ground buckets of dried corn kernels into a powdery mesh and water splashed loudly over the rotating wheel.

Despite the cloudy skies, there had been several farmers standing around. In fact, it appeared to be something of a meeting place. There was talk about a blacksmith setting up his work and someone building a dry goods store. Gazing at the field to the rear, Nellie tried to visualize the quiet countryside filled with the noise of chatter and horse drawn buggies. It would certainly be a different place.

Shaking off her thoughts, she realized that Jake was

urging her to keep up. Unfamiliar with the landscape, he had suggested that they explore the area. Venturing out on a road that led away from the mill, they had not gone far when storm clouds had gathered. Ahead, Nellie vaguely glimpsed a row of buildings. Jake had stopped at the first structure to wait for Nellie.

"We'd better try to take shelter here," his voiced raised above the downpour.

She could see a light burning through the windows that looked out onto the big covered porch. Up close, she could see that the white planked home was much nicer than the Morgan's log cabin. Jake knocked hard on the door as Nellie stood by shivering. Glancing around, she noticed high backed chairs overlooking the porch's edge and three large windows on the house's front. My, her family only had one small window on the front of their cabin!

A motion in one window caught her eye. It appeared as though someone's pale hand was holding a curtain aside. The layered cloth fell quickly back into place when Nellie looked up. The door opened after the first knock to a short, matronly lady in her late forties.

She stood back, peering at them through suspicious eyes.

"We're sorry to bother you, ma'am, but we've got caught in the storm. Would you mind if we used your porch until the rain lets up?" Jake inquired pleasantly.

The woman looked from Jake to Nellie. Feeling the lady's eyes on her wet clothing, Nellie felt uncomfortably aware of how ragged she must appear. Water dripped on the porch from the hem of her dress, and she could not disguise the shiver that caused her frame to tremble.

The lady's solemn expression broke into a smile and she answered brightly, "Oh, where are my manners?" Reaching towards them, she continued, "Come on in you poor things. We'll see what we can do about your wet clothes."

"You'll catch your death out here, child," she muttered. Stepping aside, she held the open door with a hand placed on

Nellie's back.

Thankful to leave the dreary, damp outdoors, they stepped inside. Nellie was taken back when she glimpsed their fine surroundings. A kerosene lamp threw a golden glow on one side of the room that held a fireplace in the corner. A lively fire burned high with golden tipped flames. The two sources of combined light revealed a room like Nellie had never seen.

The ivory walls were painted in tiny sprigs of lilac flowers and pale pink rose buds. Standing out against the pretty background were pieces of furniture wearing fancy crocheted doilies. The place didn't look lived in at all, unlike the Morgan home that was filled with the clutter of seven people.

With a hand on Nellie's back, the lady prodded her towards the warm fire. While she and Jake stood warming themselves, the lady hurried off to get towels. Hearing a light step, Nellie turned to see a tall, slender girl in the doorway. Her blond curls were in disarray around her face. Despite her just-woke-up appearance, she was a pretty girl. Her dark blue eyes studied them slowly before she smiled.

"Hello," the girl spoke softly.

"Hello," Nellie returned.

"I don't believe we've met before," she greeted, extending her hand to Nellie, while looking boldly at Jake.

"No, I don't think so," Nellie replied.

"Hi there," broke in Jake's deeper and more masculine voice. Reaching forward, he took the initiative, extending his large, roughened hand.

"Why hello," the girl breathed softly in a voice resembling a whisper.

Bustling back into the room, the older woman announced, "Oh, I see you've met my daughter, Elizabeth May."

Sizing Nellie up with squinted eyes, she added, "and I think you two girls must be about the same age. How old are you, honey?"

When she answered that she was fifteen, the lady clapped her hands in delight.

"Oh, Elizabeth! We've finally found someone your own age."

Peering back at Nellie, she continued, "My, we've been here for nearly a year now, and we had given up hope of finding someone Elizabeth could befriend." Excited, she asked, "Pray tell, where have you been hiding?"

The lady wanted to know where she lived. Nellie didn't know exactly how to answer. Where did she live? How could she explain that she lived in a small cabin in the middle of nowhere? She was thankful when Jake spoke for her. He explained that the Morgan's home was located about six miles west of Dan's mill.

The half-hour they were inside passed quickly, for the lady they came to know as Mrs. Hallie, liked to talk. When the rain had stopped to a drizzle, they said their good byes. Mrs. Hallie urged them to stay longer, warning them of the fog laying low in the trees. Jake politely refused, saying that they should be heading back before it darkened.

"You'll please come again, won't you?" Elizabeth implored sweetly.

Before leaving, they agreed.

As autumn passed, Nellie visited Elizabeth May several times with Jake's as an escort. During these visits, Jake chose to go along to the mill in order to catch up with other farmers while she and Elizabeth engaged in what he called *girl-talk*.

Although she and her new found friend didn't have an awful lot in common, Nellie found the other girl quite interesting. While Elizabeth's soft appearance and lady-like attire made Nellie feel slightly rough around the edges, she still enjoyed drinking tea in what Mrs. Hallie called the "parlor".

There was also a wall of books that Mrs. Hallie had insisted she read. Allowed to borrow as many as she could carry home at one time, Nellie had taken the woman up on the offer. Reading out loud to her little sisters, they, too, had come to enjoy the adventures found between the covers. Each time the books were finished, they begged for more.

Although it had taking a bit of getting used to, Nellie had to admit that it was actually nice to have a female friend who was close in age. She soon discovered that Elizabeth May was not the quiet person she had first judged her to be. In fact, the giggling girl always wore a smile and loved to tease. Nellie found herself laughing a lot in Elizabeth May's company and often carried a smile home with her.

The six miles to her friend's home seemed to grow shorter with each visit. She soon discovered that traveling by horseback reduced the trip to an hour and a half. Nellie remembered the first time she had arrived at Elizabeth's doorstep on horseback. Her friend had been amazed that she could control such a big animal. Elizabeth had never ridden a horse, and she and her mother traveled the area by buggy.

Often, her friend spoke of the town she had left behind which was quite different from living in the backwoods. Nellie didn't quite understand what she meant by *backwoods* since there weren't that many trees around Elizabeth's house, and her home sat within sight of three others.

The town Elizabeth described seemed like a place out of the books she had borrowed. Nellie wondered if she would ever see the brick roads and lanterns swinging from poles that stood along the streets. In an excited voice, Elizabeth promised that someday she'd take Nellie to the place she used to live.

One day, the two were walking to the pump for water when Elizabeth, again, caught Nellie off-guard.

"Nellie, how do you feel about Jake? What's it like living so close to him?"

Stunned, Nellie stammered, "What?"

"I mean, how can you possibly *not* fall in love with him? He has that sparkle in his dark eyes when he smiles, and that incredible, husky voice nearly drives me mad! He has got to be the most handsome man I've ever seen!" she finished dreamily. "Whenever he's around, I simply can't take my eyes off him!"

Nellie licked her dry bottom lip before replying carefully,

"Well...he is attractive. But we're together so much that he just seems like family. He's like a brother to me."

Elizabeth looked skeptical, but she didn't say anything more. Nellie quickly changed the subject. Her friend's bold declaration remained in her thoughts long after being spoken. The admission would have been forgotten if Jake had continued remaining at the mill when Nellie went along to visit her friend. It wasn't long before she noticed a change in his expression when Elizabeth's name was mentioned.

While they were both at Elizabeth's house one evening, Nellie observed Jake from the corner of her eye. It was apparent that he was somewhat smitten with her friend. His admiring gazes and deep, rich laughter could not go unnoticed. In turn, Elizabeth was finding every opportunity to touch him playfully on the arm as she commented in a teasing fashion. Nellie felt a tight pull in her chest. Suddenly she wished that she had never met her golden hair friend.

Walking towards the door, she cleared her throat. "If you two won't mind, I'm going to check on Breeze."

Jake looked up briefly, nodding. She doubted that Elizabeth noticed her departure. The other girl was busy spinning some story of mischief.

She stepped out onto the porch. Neither looked up as she left. In those moments, Nellie felt a rush of loneliness wash over like nothing she had experienced in fifteen years. Walking absently over to Breeze, she began to rub the gelding's neck. The animal's gentle neigh gave her a warm feeling of belonging. At least someone cared for her, even if he was only a horse.

She might just head on home. Jake would be along soon. Instead of heading straight to the cabin, she took the long way around. The further she traveled from Elizabeth May's house, the better she felt. Nellie didn't want to be around anyone right now, not even family. Turning Breeze in the opposite direction of her home, it was not long before they came to the river. On impulse, she nudged the gelding onward, never losing sight of the river's banks.

She continued riding until she began to feel numb from the dropping temperature. Night was falling, and she had never come this far late in the day. The cold air was chilly, and she was thankful for the fur coat that she had thrown over her shoulders earlier in the day. Despite its protection around her upper body, Nellie could not ward off the numbness seeping into her fingers and toes.

Coming to a valley between two bluffs, she brought the gelding to a halt when she could barely see the forest before her. Breeze, too, would not know where to step in the dark. Raking back the damp leaves, she lay down on a spot of dry ground. For insulation, Nellie pulled her fur coat over her body and decided that this would be her resting place for the night. There was no way she could continue any further in the dark.

She lay there, breathing in her cupped hands for warmth. Somehow she managed to lightly doze, but it wasn't long before she awakened, miserable and freezing. Her teeth chattered uncontrollably, and she massaged her nearly frost bitten toes with numb fingers. Nellie knew that she must move to keep her blood circulating. A frost had covered the forest, and she could feel its moisture penetrating both her skin and clothing.

Taking Breeze by the reins, she walked cautiously through the woods, trying to dodge trees and other objects concealed in her path. The night was pitch black, and her only guide was the sound of the river to her far left. With each step, Nellie was comforted in knowing that a cozy bed and warm fire awaited her arrival. Guiltily, she knew that her family must be worried sick when she had not come home.

The return journey seemed to take forever, and she could barely recognize familiar surroundings in the dark. Slowing her pace, she halted, deciding to seek the horse's frame for warmth. Standing close, Nellie circled her arms about Breeze's neck, and nestled her face into the gelding's warm neck. Nellie was surprised at how comfortable she became. She chastised herself for not thinking of the idea earlier.

She lodged against the gelding for what seemed like

hours and several times she had to catch herself from falling as she nodded off to sleep. Nellie held this stance until daybreak, when the morning light revealed that they were actually closer to the cabin than she had thought. In fact, they were nearly within sight of the oak tree where she had first met Jake.

Climbing quickly onto Breeze, she coaxed the horse into a trot. Beginning to slowly thaw, she was nearly overcome with fatigue when she caught her first glimpse of the cabin. Never had she been so glad to see her rustic log home with its smoke curling from the chimney!

The beagle's barking announced her arrival. Nellie stopped short when she noticed a tall figure striding toward her in a determined march across the field. It was Jake! Nearly running, he hurried to meet her before she could reach the barn. Anger mixed with anxiety showed on his face. For a fleeting moment, he looked far more like the stranger that she remembered.

Nellie slipped off the gelding indifferently, hoping Jake would not make a big scene. With sparks of anger flashing in his eyes, he burst forth angrily.

"Nell, are you all right? Where have you been? You've had your parents worried sick! Your pa has stayed out half the night looking for you! He's now in bed with a cold and sore throat. He hollered your name until he could barely speak."

He grabbed hold of Nellie's shoulders, shaking her body as he spoke. She saw shadows under his eyes and tension around his mouth. Of course, he didn't look much worse than she must have appeared. She fingered the hem of her coat, staring at the ground. The grueling past few hours, along with Jake's outburst, was taking its toll.

Nellie started to sniffle, tears sliding down her cheeks. As her quiet sniffles escalated into sobs, she could not disguise the trembling that shook her frame. Jake stood by, speechless.

Apparently regretting his harsh tone, he pulled her tightly to his chest. His fingers entwined absently in her hair, as he whispered soothingly, "I'm sorry, Nellie. Please forgive me.

Lord knows, I wouldn't hurt you for the world."

When her sobs ceased, Jake said in a hoarse voice, "I was so worried about you. When I didn't find you outside Elizabeth's, I thought you had come back here. I really couldn't think of where you would have gone without telling me first. When I came back, you weren't here, and your folks thought you were with me." He paused, and continued, "We thought you'd be along any time, but when you still hadn't come back this morning, I was going crazy. Something must have happened to you, and probably you were too hurt to call for help."

He looked at Nellie intently and finished, "Please don't ever scare me like that again." He sighed, placing a hand on her shoulder. "I didn't mean to make you cry. Forgive me?" he asked huskily, bringing her chin up so that her eyes met his.

Nellie nodded, and Jake gave her a warm hug. She stepped away.

Someone must have heard Jake speaking for her mother called out.

"Nellie! Are you all right, honey?"

Martha walked quickly, carrying a blanket in her arms.

"Here, dear," she soothed, wrapping her daughter in the soft, flannel folds.

Pa stepped forward, wearing an expression much like Jake's had been. What had kept her out all night, he wanted to know.

She answered only with a shrug of her shoulders. What could she possibly tell her parents? At the moment, she could think of no logical answer so she remained silent.

Martha put an arm around her husband's back, speaking in a low tone, "Now you know Nellie must be really tired. She can talk to us after she has rested."

Joseph lowered his shoulders, speaking gruffly, "We'll talk about this later. You'll have some explaining to do. Come on now, let's not wake up your brother and sisters."

Taking a deep breath, Nellie knew that she should get this over with. Looking at her pa, she said simply, "I know this may

48

not make sense to you, but I just had to get away. I started out riding with every intention of getting back before dark. Night just fell all at once, and I was too far away to see my way back."

Patting her horse on the neck, she continued, "I can thank Breeze, here, for keeping me from getting too cold during the night. I leaned against him to stay warm."

Joseph was getting slightly red in the face, and she knew that her explanation was not the one he had expected to hear. Concern was written in the tiny lines that were becoming more evident on her mother's forehead, yet she remained silent.

"You knew it would be getting dark, so you should have turned back. Anything could have happened to you out there. If you had yelled for help, no one could have heard your call. How do you think your ma and I felt knowing that something could be wrong with our girl?" He reached towards his wife, while continuing, "Your being gone has really worried your ma. She didn't sleep a wink last night." He looked off into the distance and finished abruptly, "I want you to stay close to the cabin from now on. There'll be no riding or taking walks, you hear?"

Nellie nodded with slumped shoulders.

Chapter Six

Winter came as the trees lost their dying leaves. Joseph's decision to make his daughter stay at home couldn't have happened at a better time. It was actually too cold to remain outdoors for long. While she had often regretted the winter, this season gave Nellie a welcome chance to stay indoors near Jake.

The lean-to on the side of the cabin had been finished, and Jake was always with the family. Nellie and Jake often sat by the fire, engrossed in long talks. Despite their close quarters, she chose to dismiss her growing affection for him. She continued to visit Elizabeth occasionally, and Jake often came along.

The light snows that had begun to fall cut Nellie's visits short. It was a week before Christmas, and although she had not visited her friend in the past few weeks, this day had been planned. She and Elizabeth were going to exchange gifts.

Using some of her grandmother's beads, Nellie had threaded them onto a pretty blue ribbon that Elizabeth could use in her hair. The colors would be a lovely contrast with her pale, blond hair. Peering at Jake as they rode along, she wondered if he had brought her friend a gift. She caught herself studying his profile in his outgrown coat that stretched tautly across his broad shoulders.

She glanced away when Elizabeth's house came into view. They were about to step up on the porch when the door opened. Elizabeth bounced out, wearing a glowing smile along with a pretty velvet, wine colored dress. As she took their coats, Nellie looked down at her own exposed gray, woolen matronly dress. The dress had been her mother's and it hung loosely on her frame.

Moving near the flames burning warmly in the fireplace, Nellie decided to forget she was wearing her old homespun dress. At least it was insulation against the cold weather.

She was pleasantly surprised to find that Mrs. Hallie had gone to a good bit of trouble in preparing for their visit. A small table had been set near the fire, arranged with appealing bite-size sweets. Although there was no tree, the window draperies and table had been decorated in elaborate emerald and red velvet material. Running cedar had been placed along the windowsills, and a single candle burned in the center of each.

Speaking to Jake in an excited whisper, Elizabeth motioned for him to step into the adjoining kitchen. Disheartened by their familiar comradeship, Nellie tried not to think about Elizabeth's wish to be alone with him.

Giggling, Elizabeth bounced cheerfully back into the room alone. Curious about what could be keeping Jake, Nellie didn't get the opportunity to ask. Mrs. Hallie bustled into the room, greeting Nellie affectionately. She inquired how the Morgans were doing this Christmas season. With the lady's constant chatter, and between nibbles, Jake was pushed to the far corner of Nellie's mind.

"Ho! Ho! Ho!" declared a deep baritone that sounded suspiciously like Jake.

Coming through the doorway to the kitchen was Jake, wearing a big, red, floppy hat from which hung a white ball of cotton. His shoulders were draped with running cedar, just like those used on the tables and windowsills. Laughter bubbled up in Nellie's throat at the foolish sight. She had never heard of such a strange costume except in books. Why, he looked downright ridiculous!

When he walked over to the fireplace where the few gifts were lying, Nellie could see that he was carrying a small bag over

51

his shoulder. He reached inside, taking one package out at a time.

After the gifts had been handed out, Nellie was surprised to find that she had received three small packages and one large one. She had only brought one present, and that had been for Elizabeth. Looking at the packages on her friend's lap and the ones at her feet, she discovered that Elizabeth had received the most gifts. Apparently, Mrs. Hallie and Elizabeth had chosen to celebrate Christmas a week early.

The small gifts that Nellie and Jake opened contained wrapped cookies and other treats. She wondered if Jake had given Elizabeth a gift. If he had, it had been in the kitchen for she didn't see anything. However, her friend did have one for him. Hearing his low whistle of admiration, Nellie could see that he had been given a fine hunting knife. It was obviously a very costly gift, for knives of that quality were rare. Jake thanked Elizabeth sheepishly, telling her that she shouldn't have done it. She waved a hand in the air, saying that it was nothing.

Nellie's large gift was wrapped in a decorated paper package similar to Jake's. Fingering the soft material, she lifted up a pretty pink dress, far more feminine than anything she had ever worn. She fingered the soft calico material, imagining what it would feel like against her skin.

Hearing a low whistle, she turned to see Jake grin. Embarrassed, she looked away.

Hoping her friend had not paid much attention to their exchange, she thanked Elizabeth kindly, adding that she couldn't wait to wear the dress. Nellie had to admit that she loved Elizabeth's gift.

Anxious, she watched as her small brown package was picked up. Suddenly it appeared common and out of place. Despite the coarse wrapping, Elizabeth seemed delighted with the blue ribbon trimmed in beads.

"Oh, I've not seen anything like it! Where ever did you find the pretty beads?"

Nellie told her the story of Great-grandmother Sarah and

her lost Indian love, Cloud Walker. Both Elizabeth and her mother sat enthralled when Nellie had finished the account. Her friend touched the beads lovingly, telling Nellie that she would treasure them always.

The evening soon came to a close as the chill outside threatened to bring snow. As she and Jake headed home, she felt a sense of pride in knowing that she had passed on her grandmother's legacy.

The week passed quickly, and all at once, it was the morning of Christmas Day. Joseph, Jake and John had cut a cedar tree that now stood tall in the Morgan's family room. Decorated in white cloth bow ties, the tree's needled top barely missed the ceiling's rafters. The entire family was sitting on the floor around the tree as Joseph leaned back in his rocking chair, preparing to read the Christmas story.

Nellie's younger sisters were chattering excitedly as they shook mystery packages that lay beneath the tree's branches. Jake sat on the floor with his elbows propped on his knees and his chin resting in his forearms. He appeared content and very much a part of their family. Feeling Nellie's gaze, he turned his head to send a tender smile. Her heart beat quickened. She smiled back.

Never one to give romance a great deal of thought, she had laughed when Elizabeth May described the flutter in her chest when she had first met Jake. Thinking her friend silly, Nellie had attributed the reaction to nervousness caused by a stranger. After all, it was not often that Elizabeth came into contact with strangers, especially men. Her world was one filled with ruffles and lace.

Despite Nellie's earlier scoff at romance, she could not deny the flutter that she felt when Jake sent her an endearing smile. Although she and Jake were as close as they'd ever been, there was nothing romantic between them now. What Jake felt for her, was the protection of an older brother. Nellie could not deny that he cared for her, but it was not the same love that a man felt for a woman.

Imagining Jake in thirty years, she pictured him wearing faded bib overalls and wiping sweat from his brow with a worn handkerchief. She saw herself walking towards him, carrying a pitcher of cold, spring water, smiling when he looked up in appreciation.

"Nellie."

Startled from her reverie, she took the mug of tea that her mother offered. Looking around, she saw that her siblings had also been given cups and were assembled at their father's feet. They were eager to hear the Christmas story. Leaning back on her elbows, Nellie closed her eyes as Joseph read from the Bible.

Now when Jesus was born in Bethlehem of Judaea in the days of Herod the king, behold, there came wise men from the east of Jerusalem,

Saying where is he that is born king of the Jews? For we have seen his star in the east, and are come to worship him.

The rocking chair creaked, as her father arose, picking up a stick that had been propped against the wall, unnoticed. Bent over the makeshift cane, he took several steps forward, continuing to read.

Although she had heard the story many times, Nellie never tired of listening to the birth of Christ. She envisioned the shepherds leaning on their staffs as they gathered around the newborn child. Always, a very big star hung high above the child's head.

The story came to an end too soon. As Joseph finished, he reminded the family that they, too, had been given the gift of life. Putting his arm around his wife and younger daughters, he said that God's gift giving did not stop with Christ. Loving them so much, He had given them one another. Wearing a smile, he concluded that God had added another member to their family, and that person was Jake.

"Now, me and your ma have a little something for each of ye. These small presents are like the ones that the wise men gave to Mary, the mother of Jesus. They are a way of showing our love, and we thank the Lord for putting us together as a family."

When her father had finished speaking, Nellie's sisters lost no time in reaching beneath the tree for presents bearing their names. Not having a lot of money, the Morgan's gifts were handmade instead of store bought or traded. Their father and mother always managed to give them each a gift that suited their individual needs and wishes.

Mary Ann jumped up in excitement when she had torn open her package, finding a rag doll. Martha had fastened small round button eyes above a smiling sewn mouth. She now brought Mary's attention to the white and red-checked, gingham dress that had been one of Mary's own. Actually, the dress had originally been Nellie's but had been handed down from sister to sister. Becoming too worn for wear, the dress had been crafted into a miniature size for the doll.

To Nellie's right, Laura was carefully placing a dainty apron around her waist, and a small straw broom was propped against the wall. She enjoyed helping her mother in the kitchen, yet their broom was twice her size, and the aprons swallowed her waist. Standing up proudly in her new attire, she began sweeping the floor beneath the tree, gathering bits of broken pine comb that had fallen from the branches.

Rebecca was absorbed in a packet of handwritten recipes that her mother had inscribed. There was also a cookie cutter in the shape of a star. Eager to begin cooking right away, Rebecca was disappointed when Martha told her that she must wait till there were no sweets in the house.

Her brother was busy examining a small bow that had been fashioned from a young sapling. Laying the bow down, he picked up a pouch containing three arrows. This, he secured on a belt at his waist. Nellie smiled, knowing that John couldn't wait to get in the woods.

Centered on a lace tablecloth, used only during special occasions, sat a two-layer pound cake, glazed with honey. On each side of the pound cake, her mother had placed small bowls of nuts, mints, and dried apple rings. The latter was disappearing quickly because the cake would not be eaten until all the gifts had been opened.

Directing her attention to Jake, Nellie now saw that he was about to open the present that she had prepared. Not knowing what to give him at first, she had thought a long time before deciding on the leather moccasins, decorated with the beaded circles. Jake looked at the moccasins, pleased. An expression fleeted across his face that Nellie could not name. She caught her breath! But it was too much to hope. He stroked the soft deerskin.

"Thank you, Nellie."

She smiled, hoping that her joy at his reaction had not been too obvious. She looked away quickly, and noticed that her mother had been watching them. She flushed, glad that she had not told her mother the meaning of the two circles.

Not expecting a gift from Jake, she was surprised when he presented her with a small brown parcel, tied in string. She tugged the knot carefully, trying not to damage the paper. Wrapped in a square shape, the paper covered a small hand-made wooden box fashioned out of pine. Nellie's mouth unconsciously opened in awe, for he must have spent hours making the box that showed the carving of a tree on its lid. Nellie thanked him, although words could never show how much the gift truly meant to her.

That night when Nellie walked outside, she heard the door open and shut again after she had stepped out. She was not alone. Crouching so that her legs hung over the porch's edge, she felt the floor boards strain under a heavier weight. She looked up to find Jake lowering himself to the porch, by her side.

The air was cold, and frost had covered the yard in a damp blanket. Nellie questioned her motives for coming outside in such miserable conditions. Unable to stop the shiver that spread over her frame, Nellie was surprised when she felt Jake's arm pulling her into the folds of his open jacket.

For a while, neither of them spoke. Oddly, there seemed to be no need for words. It was Jake who broke the silence.

"You sure have some good folks, Nellie." Taking a deep breath, he continued, "I've never spent Christmas in the way that we just did. In fact, Christmas really never was a big deal with my family. Sure we had dinner with all the trimmings, but presents were never exchanged, and I didn't have a pa to read the Christmas story to me."

He seemed rather sad, and Nellie reached to squeeze his hand.

"I'm glad you enjoyed spending this Christmas with us," she said softly.

Jake continued, "Sitting in there with all of you, I didn't feel out-of-place, even though I'm not part of the family. It's funny, but being here seems so natural...almost like I've been here forever." He paused. "Almost like this is where I'll always be."

Nellie couldn't help looking up at him as he spoke. For a brief moment, she thought she detected a fine mist in his eyes. The sky held a full moon, and its brightness couldn't disguise the unnatural sheen in his brown eyes.

Without thinking, Nellie hugged him, pulling his jacket more snugly around the two of them. Jake's hold on her tightened. Nothing could have affected Nellie so deeply. In that unguarded moment, she had witnessed a part of him that she doubted he had ever shown to anyone.

"Jake, you are a part of our family," she said gently.

She moved away from him slowly.

"I guess I'll be going in now." With a smile, she finished, "It's getting colder, and my sisters should have the bed warmed by now."

"Goodnight, Nellie," she heard Jake speak softly as she passed through the door.

Chapter Seven

Winter melted into the spring of 1861. The season brought a change that had nothing to do with the weather. There was trouble brewing in the land. It came to a peak when a tall, lanky man from Kentucky was elected President. Abe Lincoln was his name.

Siding with the people of the north, he supported laws that hurt Virginia and other southern states. It angered the farmers that they were being told what to do by men who knew nothing about raising a crop or tilling the soil.

Already, Virginia and neighboring states were breaking away from the Union. Establishing their independence, a Confederacy was being formed. They would make their own laws. This made the Union and people of the north so angry that there was talk of war.

Nellie hardly knew what to think of all this. That big word *government* seemed so far removed from their cabin in the woods, almost like it was part of another world. But it wasn't, because there were taxes to pay and all sorts of records to be kept. She knew that someday the government would own a very important document that carried her own name. It would be her marriage bond.

Imagining the man who would share his name on the document, Nellie was instantly assailed with thoughts of Jake. She tightened her lips, shaking her head. That wasn't likely to happen.

Their friendship had grown, brought on by their close quarters during the winter. Still, he treated her like a sister. But, she couldn't help harboring a hope that he would someday look at her like Pa looked at her mother.

Despite their close relationship, Nellie was shocked one day when Jake announced that he was going to visit Elizabeth May. There had been no warning and he didn't even invite her along! She was hurt.

The entire time he was gone, Nellie watched the sun travel overhead. He sure was taking a long time. The day was surprisingly warm, and felt much like summer. Why had Jake decided to visit her friend? Elizabeth's name rarely came up in their conversations, and Nellie tried to avoid any mention of her at all.

Jake made it back to the cabin just in time for supper. Nellie sat in uncomfortable silence, not talking as she normally would. Aware that Jake had been gone for the entire day, Joseph was curious.

"How was your day, Jake?"

"Oh, it went well. I took Mrs. Hallie some seeds for a small garden that she's planting behind her house. She hardly knew what to do with them, so I showed her and Elizabeth how they should be planted."

Nellie felt a bit relieved that he had not gone there for the sole reason of visiting her blond friend. Still, she didn't understand why he hadn't invited her along unless he wanted to be alone with Elizabeth May.

Nellie's thoughts drifted back to her friend's earlier comment concerning her attraction to Jake. Jealously, she wondered if Jake treated Elizabeth the same way that he treated her. Of course, that wasn't saying much. She had hoped that his affectionate gestures would come to mean more, but they had not.

If Jake noticed any change in their relationship after his visit to Elizabeth, he didn't mention it. He probably didn't have much time to think about the rift in their friendship now that his visits to the other girl were increasing. Nellie sniffed. There was only so much planting that a person could do in a tiny yard.

Because she and Jake were still together quite often, he began to speak confidentially of his sudden attraction to Elizabeth May. Funny, she couldn't see why it had taken him so long to notice her friend's encouraging looks. Nellie refused to offer any encouragement to his courtship. By simply listening, her curiosity about their growing fondness was satisfied. The warm weather soon began to keep Jake at home, for there were fields to plow.

Finding the spring time temperatures ideal for walking, the woods became a salve for Nellie's troubles. The air was cool as she traveled down the well-trodden path to the river. Her feet made thuck-thuck sounds against the leaves that had been flattened beneath the winter snows. Instinctively, she wrapped her arms over her chest, hugging her body in the battered knitted sweater that had been handed down for generations.

As she walked along, her thoughts turned inward. She could not help thinking about Jake and Elizabeth May. Suddenly, she felt very left out. Since Christmas, she had not visited her friend although Jake had asked her to come along on his second visit. Nellie had declined, knowing that he was only trying to pose as an escort.

Yes, it would have seemed very appropriate. But Nellie had made some excuse, just as she had done on other occasions. She refused to sit by and watch her two friends gaze at one another.

Elizabeth always sent her "hellos" through Jake, expressing that she would like Nellie to visit. Nellie seriously doubted that her company was missed. In fact, she knew that Elizabeth would much rather be alone with Jake.

Finding that she had not gotten away from the thoughts that had driven her from the cabin, she cut the walk short. Traveling homeward, she wondered if her parents had noticed the rift that was developing around her. Worried that her family would begin to speculate about why her visits to Elizabeth May

60

had stopped, Nellie knew she should be more careful. In fact, her biggest fear was that Jake would find that she cared for him, then confide in Elizabeth May. The last thing Nellie wanted to see was pity in her friend's eyes.

Fortunately, Jake was absent when Nellie returned home. She was in no mood to see him, for she could feel the damp, tear-traces on her cheeks. Her mother looked at her with concern, worry etched on her face.

Touching her daughter's shoulder as Nellie started to brush by, she inquired, "Nellie, you were out early this morning. Is everything okay?"

"Yes, I guess."

She couldn't hide the sadness in her voice.

"Are you sure? You have been staying to yourself a lot lately. We miss you." She smiled softly, giving Nellie a gentle hug.

Quick to ease her mother's mind, she reassured with, "I'm fine, Ma. I've just been feeling a bit under the weather lately."

At the worry in her mother's eyes, she continued, "No, it's not what you think. When I say that I feel under the weather, I'm not talking about being sick."

Martha raised her eyebrows and asked quietly, "Would this have something to do with Jake and Elizabeth May?"

Startled at her mother's keen observance, she could only stammer, "What do you mean?"

Looking at her daughter with endearment, she took a deep breath, and began to explain.

"I was 23 when your father came into my life. Up until the time we met, I had never been courted. There were many young men in the town where I lived, but I was very shy. When my friends gained attention from their admirers, they were quick to step forward. They were soon married, while I hung back, alone.

I met your father when he came through town selling farm goods. He was a mature 30 year-old who saw beyond my quiet manner. We soon became friends, for your father had a way of making people talk." She smiled, as she continued, "After our first meeting, he began calling on me. It was about six months later that he finally asked my father's permission to have my hand in marriage." She laughed softly, "Those six months were the longest months of my life. I thought your father took forever in asking me to be his wife!"

Nellie had never known how her father and mother had met. She had never thought to ask. She had forgotten that her mother had lived in a town like Elizabeth May. Of course, her mother and Elizabeth were nothing alike.

"Your father and I were friends from the start. Although I missed my parents when we moved away, it was made easier because my husband was my friend." She looked thoughtfully at her daughter and finished, "You and Jake have become very good friends. When I see the two of you together, I am reminded of your father and me. Perhaps you didn't expect Jake's interest in Elizabeth May to affect your friendship, but I can see that it has."

As she listened to her mother, Nellie examined the boards at her feet. What could she say? Taking a deep breath, she said quietly, "I didn't plan to feel this way about him. We make a great team when we're working together, and he has become like the older brother I never had. It's just that recently, I feel like my trust has been betrayed. What if he tells Elizabeth May the things we've talked about?" She sighed. "Elizabeth probably thinks that I sure have a big head for a country girl."

Martha gave her daughter a soothing look, "Oh, honey, you don't have a big head, and I'm sure Jake will not discuss your private conversations with Elizabeth." She paused, and continued carefully, "I believe you're worried about more than Jake betraying your trust. I think it won't be too long before Jake discovers that he and Elizabeth May have very little in common.

Elizabeth is mysterious and new to him. He doesn't see her as much as he does you. When he gets to know her better, he will be more able to decide whether he really wants to pursue a relationship beyond friendship. Time will tell." She squeezed Nellie's shoulders lightly. "Just be patient with him."

Still in Martha's arms, Nellie hugged her mother tightly. It was reassuring to know that she wasn't alone.

"Thank you, Ma. I'm glad you understand." She smiled, tears shining in her eyes.

Suddenly her mother exclaimed, "Oh Nellie! Have you forgotten that your sixteenth birthday is only three weeks away?"

She had almost forgotten. Sixteen was a special age. It was a time when a little girl became a woman. There was no schoolwork, and it was an age when a woman began to look for a spouse. With a start, Nellie realized that people would expect her to begin planning for the future. Not willing to think that far ahead, she closed her mind to the thought of marriage. She didn't want to think that Elizabeth May must be thinking along the same lines.

"Nellie, why don't you go wake the children up for breakfast?" Martha asked as she began setting the table.

Heading up the ladder, Nellie felt like a weight had been lifted from her shoulders. She was happy that her mother understood. Feeling much lighter by the time she reached the top step, she practically hopped across the room. Shaking her sisters gently awake, she sank to the bed, hugging all three at once.

While they were getting dressed, she hurried out to find John. He was coming from the hen house, carrying a basket of eggs. She looked up at her brother now. Over the winter, he had grown quite a few inches. He was growing tall and she was careful not to pick fights with him as she had done when they were younger.

Looking at the barnyard behind him, she could see that fresh hay had been put down for the cattle. Jake and John must have been at work early since her father was just shaving when she passed by.

"Where's Jake? Is he coming in for breakfast?"

John pointed to the woods behind the field.

"No, he left early this morning. Said there was something he needed to do. He took a satchel that looked pretty full. Think it was food. Told me to tell Pa and Ma that he was going to visit his folks, but he'd be coming back."

Stunned, Nellie stared towards the road's bed.

"Did he say where they live?"

"No, but it must be a ways. Said he'd be gone for a few days."

Curious, she wondered why Jake had left without telling anyone. Jake hadn't told her that he was going anywhere, either. Of course, they hadn't talked as much lately. But it seemed that he would have mentioned a thing like going to visit his family.

Suddenly, she was worried. What if he was going home to prepare his uncles for a new member to the family? Could it be that Jake was thinking of asking for Elizabeth's hand in marriage? Every man had to have a surety's signature on his marriage bond. This was another person who would be legally responsible for the debt that it cost to marry. Usually this was a father or close member of the family. In Jake's case, it would be one of his uncles.

She bit her lip. Swallowing the tears that threatened to fall, she shook her head with determination. No! It couldn't be true. Jake and Elizabeth had nothing in common. Anyone could see that.

With eyes squeezed tightly shut, Nellie uttered a silent prayer. *Please Lord, don't let it be so. But if it's your will, please give me strength!*

Swallowing the lump in her throat, she pushed away the wave of loneliness that threatened to overtake her. She *had* to believe that things were not as they seemed.

64

Chapter Eight

Following her father's plow, Nellie picked up stones that had fallen from the over-turned earth. Frowning in her thoughts, she wondered when Jake was planning to return. He had been gone for a week. Wiping the perspiration from her forehead with the sleeve of her dress, she was startled at their dog's warning barks. Dropping the rocks to a nearby pile, she flicked dirt from her fingers. The dog's insistent barks could only mean company.

She looked up as an open horse drawn wagon stopped near the barn. Squinting, she could see a figure wearing a broad rimmed hat, shielding the face from recognition. With one hand held tightly to the wagon's seat, the small, angular frame swung lightly to the ground. Nellie was curious when the figure disappeared around the barn. Who was this person?

Afraid to bring attention to herself, she whistled lightly to her father who was plowing with the mule. When he did not respond, she ran towards him quickly. Trying to get his attention, she waved her arms. He looked up, agitated at her frantic movements.

"Nellie, what in the world are you doing?"

She held a finger over her lips, making a motion that he stop. Pulling back on the mule's tether, he brought the animal to a stand still. He was about to comment again when his eye caught the unfamiliar wagon.

"Now, who do we have here?" he muttered, more to himself than to Nellie.

"Pa, that's why I've been trying to get your attention. Someone's here. I saw him get off the wagon, and go around the barn."

Dropping the mule's tether, Joseph picked up a stick and began walking briskly towards the barn. Following close behind, Nellie was surprised to hear Mary Ann's excited giggle. She looked briefly at the wagon's contents as she passed by. She could see various worn work tools, along with half a dozen sacks that were filled to the point of nearly bursting. It looked like someone was moving. Probably asking for directions. Of course, they lived off the main road, so someone was sure going out of their way.

Nellie stepped back from the wagon when she heard her father's hearty welcoming tone. Eager to know what was going on, she stepped into view. At once, she heard the husky masculine voice that she had come to know well. It was Jake! And standing by his side was the man she had seen hop from the wagon. Very similar to Jake in features, he was probably older by twenty years.

"Hey, Nellie. Sure have missed you." Jake came forward to give her a big hug. Pulling away, he continued, "And look who I've brought back. This is my Uncle Bill."

Giving Jake a brotherly pat on the back, the little man stepped forward, holding his hat in his hand.

"Nice to meet you, ma'am."

"Uncle Bill has come along to help me build my own place." He looked at Nellie's parents as he continued, "You folks have been really good to me, but it's time I got out on my own."

Uncle Bill looked at Nellie's parents in appreciation as he spoke, "Jake has told me a lot of good things about you folks. You've taken good care of my boy."

"Oh, it works both ways. Young Jake has been taking care of us, too. I would've never gotten all of last year's crop if it hadn't been for his help," Joseph said with a nod.

Jake shook his head, smiling, "I was just glad that I could be around. You gave me a place to live, treating me like I was a

66

part of the family. I couldn't have asked for more."

He pointed now in the direction at the far corner of the field.

"I've met the man who owns the land back there. With a little bit of money that I've been saving, I bought a hundred and thirty acres that joins yours. Uncle Bill is a carpenter and we've brought back his tools to build a cabin."

The three men walked towards the wagon, discussing the kind of structure that would be built. Jake was very excited about some of the cabin's features, and it was clear that his uncle was very experienced in woodcraft. Jake's place would be more detailed than their small home.

Nellie had not expected Jake to move away so soon. She had never really given thought to the idea that he would someday leave. Of course, he had only been with them for a little more than a year. That short time had seemed like a lifetime to her.

Feeling a sinking sensation in her heart, Nellie knew what this must mean. Men only built homes when they were ready to fill them with a family. Jake's determination to establish his own place could only mean that he planned to take a wife. That person could only be Elizabeth May.

Jake and his uncle did not waste time in planning out the cabin. On the next day, he and Bill were crouched over a bare place on the ground when Nellie walked by. Using a stick, Jake drew an outline of his future home and was adding a separate shed to the yard.

He looked up when Nellie approached, smiling.

"Look at this and tell me what you think." Pointing at the markings, he said, "There's a big room, here, with a fireplace, giving me lots of room for company. And there'll be two big windows overlooking the river so I can feel like I'm outdoors even when I'm inside."

While he continued to describe the place, Nellie remembered that she had once shared her own ideas of a dream home. Her log cabin would have a rock fireplace that nearly covered an entire wall, she had said. This idea had come about after she and Jake had been caught in the rain that had led them to Mrs. Hallie's cozy fire. She had realized, then, that all homes were not alike.

Getting up to his feet, Jake grabbed Nellie's hand.

"Come on, let's go for a walk. Bill, I'm going to show Nellie where I'm thinking of building the cabin."

"Go right ahead. I've got some last minute planning to do before we can start tomorrow," Bill motioned for the pair to go.

They entered the woods, and it wasn't long before they reached the river. When Jake turned to head down stream, she looked at her surroundings with renewed interest. She had spent much of her time up the river, and had not traveled too much down stream.

They had been walking for thirty minutes when Nellie noticed that the river was no longer in view, although its rambling rush could still be heard. They had been steadily climbing a hill, and Nellie was unprepared for the view at the top. What she would have guessed to be a steep bluff, was actually a large hill that overlooked the river.

Stopping as he spread out his arms, Jake asked, "So, what do you think, Nell? Isn't this beautiful?"

"It's perfect," she sighed.

Closing her eyes, she imagined a cabin sitting high on the river's bank. It would be surrounded by hardwood trees and appear very much a part of the forest. The small yard would be edged with ferns and flowering orange cowbells.

"I'm glad you like it."

Taking Nellie by the hand, he pointed towards the river with his forefinger.

"You know the big room I showed you? It's going to be at the back of the house, instead of at the front like you'd think. There'll be windows on the wall that face the river, and I'm going to build a porch that will overlook the river, too. I'll sit out there at night, listening to the water and the crickets." He grinned.

Walking to the spot that began to slope down towards the

river, Jake gestured to a large maple near the hill's edge.

"This is the spot where the big room will be. The shade will keep the place cool in the summer, and a swing can be attached to that limb." He gestured, pointing towards a branch hanging about seven feet from the ground.

"That'll be nice, " Nellie murmured.

Of course, she couldn't help thinking that Jake could only be putting a swing there for small children. Turning abruptly, she stepped away from him. Climbing onto a huge rock that jutted out beyond the hill, Nellie sat down with her legs hanging over the edge.

Crunching leaves announced that Jake was close behind. Climbing up to crouch by her side, he filled the remaining space on the rock. Her pulse quickened when she felt his body settle closely against her side. Feeling the subtle movement of his breathing, Nellie could not concentrate.

With no warning, he took her chin gently in his hand. Turning her face to meet his questioning eyes, he asked, "Hey, what's wrong, Nell?"

She looked down at the river rushing below them, not giving him an answer. But before the silence could grow too awkward, she gave him a timid smile. Aware of his warm touch against her skin, Nellie placed a reassuring hand on his arm. She felt Jake's breathing lightly touch her face when he spoke softly.

"There's something about you, Nellie, that makes me feel like I've known you forever. But lately, you've been treating me like a stranger. Is it something I've said or done?" He sighed, putting his arm around her as he finished, "Because you know that I'd never do anything to hurt you."

"No, you haven't done or said anything to bother me. It's just that I'm going to miss you when you're gone. You've become a part of our family, and the place won't feel right without you." She smiled gently and added, "Now who's going to listen to me when I talk about the changing seasons or the clouds on a stormy day?" Teasing him now, she added, "And who's going to carry me to a willow hide-away, abandoning me for wild berries?"

"Now, wait a minute," he interrupted with mock chivalry. "I didn't choose the berries over you. If you remember, I brought the berries to you, and you enjoyed them just as much as I did."

Returning her playful manner, his nose intentionally bumped hers, and she felt a quick, moist peck on her cheek. At any other time, she would have been startled; instead, she affectionately nestled her face against the warm column of his throat, feeling the pulsing of his heartbeat.

Relaxing against him, she asked, "When do you plan to have the cabin finished?"

"By early fall, if everything goes well. We're going to start putting down the rocks tomorrow. I plan to have the frame built before your pa's harvest. Bill and I are going to help him with the field work, since he's giving us both a place to live."

He eased away from her now.

"I guess we'd better be getting back. Bill and I are going to make a trip back out here to gather as many rocks as we can find."

She got up with a reluctance that she hoped he wouldn't notice.

"Yes, you've got a lot to do, and I really appreciate you making the time to bring me out here."

"Well, I couldn't get started until I'd shown you the place. I'm glad you like it."

Their walk back to the cabin only took minutes. Nellie left Jake with his uncle, feeling good about the day.

In the following days, Joseph, Nellie and John helped Jake and his uncle work on the cabin's frame. She need not have worried that Jake's new home would take him away from her. If anything, it brought them closer together.

Of course, there wasn't much room for private conversation when the men's talk focused on the rebellion that was taking place. The country was divided, and there had already been some battles in northern Virginia and Missouri.

Jake's uncle spat on the ground, grinding his spittle with

70

the heel of his boot.

"Them blamed Yankees have gone too far this time! And they're goin' to get what's coming to 'em. No man's goin' to stand back while them buzzards swarm in their houses, taking what they can get, and scaring their poor women and younguns near to death."

Joseph nodded quickly in agreement. It frightened Nellie to see her father become so worked up over a cause that was so far away from them. Why, they were said to be fighting for their livelihood, but she couldn't see what that meant to her family. After all, they lived off the land.

There was talk of the colored folk getting in control if the Yankees had their way, and Nellie didn't see why that could be a worry. Why, she had only seen a few coloreds in her entire life. There certainly couldn't be many of them and what did it matter if they shared a part of the government. After all, they were part of the country, too.

Although she kept her opinion quietly to herself, Nellie didn't blame the colored folks from wanting to be free. Hadn't her country wanted to be free of the British in the 1700's? Of course, the Revolution had fixed that problem, and it looked like history was just repeating itself.

She wondered what Jake really thought of all this talk. He seemed to agree with his uncle, although he didn't use the same sense of vehemence when he spoke of the war. Nellie was growing tired of their talk and looked up in gratitude when she heard her sisters' excited chatter. What could be bringing them out here? It wasn't mid-day yet, and their mother would usually have been giving them lessons.

Caught off-guard, Nellie broke into a smile when they began singing.

Happy Birthday to you--
Happy Birthday to you--
Happy Birthday, dear Nellie-----
Happy Birthday to you!

Beaming with surprise, she had forgotten that the day was

her birthday! The men didn't seem to be caught off-guard, and as her family came forward with birthday hugs, she noticed a figure standing apart from the rest of the group. It was Elizabeth May! She came forward when the last hug had been given.

"Thought I'd never see you again, Nell! When Jake told me that a party was being planned for you, I had to come. I can see now that you've been hard at work. And it sure is sweet of you and your family to help Jake out."

The look Elizabeth sent her was one of gratitude, and Nellie felt slightly sick. How could she have forgotten about Elizabeth? She and her family were not only helping Jake, but they were also helping Elizabeth!

Attempting to appear cheerful, despite the sudden empty feeling in her stomach, Nellie smiled with false gaiety, suggesting that they help her mother who was spreading a cloth over the leaves. Throughout the next hour, Nellie kept a light banter with her guest, despite the obvious friendly nature between Jake and Elizabeth.

"I hardly ever see either of you anymore, now that you're spending all of your time on this cabin. I thought that surely I would be seeing more of you, come spring time." She addressed both of them, while giving Jake a teasing smile.

"I can see that Jake has been keeping you busy, Nellie. Really, you shouldn't let him take all of your time. He knows that you have other friends." Giving Jake a look of disapproval, she nudged him playfully as she spoke.

"Oh, Elizabeth, you know that I have been talking about building my own place all winter." Jake looked at Nellie in apology as he added, "I just didn't want to say anything to you, Nell, because I thought you might think that I haven't appreciated all that your family has done for me."

Flicking a braid over her shoulder, Nellie spoke, nonchalantly, "Well, that's understandable."

Giving Jake a look of affection, she directed her gaze to Elizabeth when she continued, "You see, we were getting used to having Jake around after he helped Pa build a room onto the cabin."

"You said you were living in the barn!" Elizabeth turned to Jake in an accusing tone.

"Well, I lived in the barn when we first met," he answered defensively.

"So how long have you been living in their home?" she retorted.

"Since this past fall," he replied.

"You mean that you've been living there the entire time we've been seeing one another?" Pausing in her accusation, she changed her voice to a tone of understanding, "Of course, I can see why you're moving out now. It must have been quite some change going from peace and quiet to a place filled with noise." Stopping when she realized that she had gone too far, she gave Nellie a look of apology.

"Oh, I didn't mean that like it sounded. It's just that I can imagine how it would be if suddenly I had a large family of younger brothers and sisters. I'm sure it was such a change for Jake when he was used to his privacy."

Before she could say more, Jake interrupted.

"No, it isn't like you think. You forget that I'm from a big family myself. My uncles were like brothers to me, and when they married, I got lots of nieces and nephews. Our place was much like Nellie's. In fact, I feel quite at home with Nellie and her family."

He gave Nellie an affectionate pat on the shoulder, and said, "Isn't that right, birthday girl?"

Returning Jake's gesture with a playful punch on the arm, she answered, "Right".

Watching their friendly exchange, Elizabeth spoke abruptly, "Well, Jake will be making a home for himself now. And who knows, maybe it won't be long before his home sounds a lot like yours." She smiled sweetly, and Nellie wanted to wipe the smirk off her face, for she knew what Elizabeth's comment implied.

That night, Nellie shifted restlessly as she lay in bed. The start of her sixteenth year was nothing like she would have planned. Her family had been wonderful in making the occasion special, yet she couldn't get Elizabeth's remarks off her mind.

Hugging her knees tightly against her chest, she cried softly. Feeling a loss that she couldn't express, she closed her eyes in attempt to shut out the darkened world around her. But rest evaded Nellie, and it wasn't until the wee hours of the morning that she finally succumbed to a fitful sleep.

Chapter Nine

Jake's cabin went up quickly. Nellie's participation in the building had gradually slackened off when the labor required a much stronger back. For once, she was glad to have her weaker femininity as an excuse.

By the end of August, the cabin was complete and Jake had moved out. His Uncle Bill had left, promising to return again. He would be going to fight the Union in the northern part of the state. There were some final preparations to make before his trek to the battle front.

"I mean to teach them dang Yanks a lesson," he had declared, stabbing his finger in the air at each word.

The days seemed to drag by for Nellie, and she found herself looking up at the approach of a horse. Disappointed, she often found that the rider was none other than her father or brother. She hoped that Jake hadn't left with his uncle. She remembered Bill's compelling tone when he spoke of a real man's duty to fight for his home front, hinting that Jake should take a stand.

While exploring the woods had once been a pleasure, Nellie now worried that Jake may think she had other reasons for the walks. What if he thought her excursions were only excuses to see him? So, when she took long walks now, she was careful to keep his home out of range.

Treading carefully amongst the thickets of briars and undergrowth, she was approaching an abandoned homestead that had never been finished. This wasn't her first visit to the site because she had seen the place while scouting with John and her pa. It had been in the fall two years back. They had been searching for deer signs such as scrapings and droppings.

The scrapings were places on the ground where the buck had brushed aside leaves to show the ground. He marked his territory by placing his hoof in the bare soil. When an interested female came along, she placed her hoof mark alongside his. This was a sign that she was ready to court. To the hunter, scrapings and deer' droppings were always a good indicator of the animal's location.

Nellie was cautiously stepping clear of a cluster of thorns when she heard her name sounding from an area of the homestead that was covered in vines.

"Nellie. Hey, girl! What are you doing out here?"

Startled, she looked up to find Jake squatting over something on the ground. What was he doing, she wondered. Carefully making her way towards him, she peered over his hunched shoulders.

"What's the matter?" she asked.

He settled back on his heels, giving her a better view of the wounded deer at his feet. The young fawn had obviously been caught in a rusty trap that was lying by its side.

"My!" exclaimed Nellie, "You saved that poor deer's life."

On hearing her voice, the animal gave a start, frantically kicking out its front legs in an attempt to get up.

"Easy," whispered Jake, stroking the fawn's neck while holding the creature down at the same time.

"How did you know about this place?" asked Nellie.

"Oh, I came across it last summer when I was passing through. Thought I'd come back to check on something extra for my cabin. The inside of the place looks pretty secure. There's a nice old mantle over the fireplace that looks as if it was carried in from some place far away. It's too nice to have been made around here."

Nellie had never been inside. Her father had warned that

the structure might not be too sturdy. She hadn't bothered to find out if he was right. Jake rose up, and the deer began its helpless struggle to move.

"He'll be okay for a few minutes. He won't be going anywhere on his own."

Jake pushed aside the tangled undergrowth, pressing the weeds down with his boot-clad foot. Taking Nellie's hand, he guided her carefully through the clearing that he had formed. At the open doorway, he took a knife from his side, and hacked away the vines that obscured the opening.

"Here," he said, gesturing toward the entrance, indicating that she should go first.

When Nellie's eyes became accustomed to the dim interior, she could see that the room was bare. The floor was dusty and strewn with leaves that had blown in from outside. The room was musty, causing her to cough when the air entered her lungs.

"Looks like this place hasn't been touched in years. I wonder why it was abandoned," she said distantly.

"I don't know, but it seems like they planned on staying here a while." Leading the way into the adjoining room, he added, "See what they've got in here."

An unfinished stairway, unlike the ladder leading up to Nellie's loft, was lying on its side. Above it, a large square opening in the ceiling seemed to lead into an attic room that could not be fully seen from the floor.

Jake had walked to the far wall where daylight streamed through a window. Tapping his knuckles on the horizontal ledge of a dark mantle propped above a fireplace, Jake said, "Now, what do you think of this beauty?"

"It could use a good dusting," she smiled. Stepping forward, Nellie admired the intricately carved wooden structure. She reached out, touching the winding grooves, tracing her index finger along the indentations. Someone had certainly put a lot of care and hours into the design.

"My! I've never seen anything like it."

"Yeah, it's a fine piece of work. It would look nice against my rocked wall. And if it's left here, it will rot over time. This house won't stand forever. I don't think anyone would mind if I gave it a good home."

"It would be perfect."

Nellie had been in Jake's cabin only a couple of times since it had been finished. On one occasion, her mother had prepared a big meal of chicken and dumplings served with fresh vegetables from their garden. When the Morgans had shown up at his door, Jake had been taken back. He had apologized for not having a table to hold all the dishes when he saw the food in their arms. They had eaten, sitting on the porch, holding their plates in their laps.

"You have a far away look in your eyes. What are you thinking?" he asked.

Nellie had not heard him come up behind her, and she felt his breath lightly touch her neck. Her pulse quickened, and she tried not to stammer when she answered.

"Oh, I was just thinking about your cabin. Do you have a table yet?"

He chuckled. The sound was low in his throat, causing Nellie to catch her breath. She turned away quickly.

"Now, why would I need a table when I have a lap?"

He leaned forward, lightly grazing her cheek with the back of his hand.

"A table wouldn't be much use for one person, now would it?" he added softly.

Nellie could think of nothing to say. She was aware of his closeness, and stiffened slightly when Jake pulled her gently against his chest. He cradled her frame, and she gradually allowed herself to relax, leaning back into his hold. Closing her eyes, she felt the rise and fall of his chest. Despite her initial awkwardness, she felt a wave of contentment sweep through her.

"Nellie," he whispered hoarsely. "I've missed seeing you so often. Why haven't you come to visit?"

She lay her head against his shoulder, answering softly,

78

"We've been busy with the garden. With the weather so nice, the weeds are having a time. John and I have been hoeing them down the minute they crop up. They're taken care of for now. That's how come I had the chance to get away."

"I should have stopped by," he said. "I could've helped you get rid of them."

"That's nice of you, but we did okay. Weeding is just part of gardening. We do it every year," she remarked.

"Still if you need my help, always know that you can give me a holler."

Jake loosened his hold, and Nellie stepped slowly away. She could sense his reluctance to part when his hand remained on her shoulder as they walked from the room.

Outside, she remembered the deer. Aware of their presence, the fawn made a half-hearted attempt to rise. Jake knelt down, shrugging off his shirt.

"I'm going to carry him back to my place. Shouldn't be long before he can stand on his own again."

She was not paying attention to his words. Instead, she was drawn to the wide expanse of his shoulders that tapered down to his narrow waist. His tall frame was of medium build, and the sinews in his back stretched as he lifted the fawn so that the shirt would work as a cradle. Tying the sleeves of his shirt together, Jake formed a knot so that carrying the small animal would be made easy.

"Guess I've got company for a while. Maybe I should build that table after all," he laughed.

They traveled together until they reached the place where Nellie was to veer off. Reaching forward to stroke the soft fur on the deer's neck, she said soothingly, "Goodbye."

As she turned to go, Jake said, "Wait. Would you like to help me get the mantle up this week?"

Pleased at the opportunity to see him again so soon, she replied, "Yes."

"O.K. I'll stop by the cabin for you soon. See you then."

With a wave, he was off.

Chapter Ten

Everyday Nellie watched for Jake's arrival. One morning, intent on removing a soiled spot from her dress with lye soap, she looked up when she heard their dog's excited bark.

"Hey there, Nellie!" Jake called.

Recognizing the voice, the beagle sprang up playfully, licking Jake's hand as he walked forward. Kneeling down, Jake scratched the pet affectionately behind the ears.

"How's the fawn?" Nellie asked.

"Oh, much better. I've been keeping him inside until he's able to walk. He should be back on his feet in a few weeks."

The sound of a door opened and thudded shut.

"Hey, Jake! How's it going?"

It was her father, coming from the barn with what appeared to be a log under his arm.

"Everything's going good. Thought I'd see if I could borrow Nellie for a few hours."

Joseph lifted an eyebrow. "Oh, there's nothing to keep her here. What are you planning to do?"

Jake explained finding the mantle in the old homestead. He thought Nellie could go out with him to take it out. He was surprised at the structure's good condition and wondered if Joseph knew the person who had once owned it.

Joseph shook his head. The place had been abandoned long before he and Nellie's mother had come to the area. He speculated that the owner might have been driven away by

Indians and death.

Nellie felt uncomfortable when her father made this last comment, for it was fairly obvious that Jake was of Indian descent. Fortunately, Jake didn't appear offended and motioned towards the load Joseph carried.

"What's that you're carrying under your arm? A log?"

Apparently, her father was working on another project. He often busied himself with small creations. Only last week, Nellie remembered the swing he had made for the girls. He had used a plank for the seat, and tied both ends to a rope that hung from a limb on an apple tree.

"A honeybee log," her father answered, pointing out the hollow center.

"I'll put a bit of honey here, and the bees will be attracted to the nectar. Before long, the queen will come with all her hive, and we'll have our own little bee tree." He smiled.

Seeing that her father was anxious to carry out his plan, Nellie wrung the water from her dress as she spoke to Jake, "I'm ready when you are."

"Okay," he nodded. "We'll be going, Joseph. Can't wait to taste your honey."

The route to the neglected homestead didn't take long. She and Jake talked along the way. It was as though time had stood still since they had last worked together in the garden.

Getting the mantle out of the place was no trouble, but carrying the awkward frame was not easy. The solid structure was heavy, despite Jake carrying the bulk of the weight. Nellie strained when they crossed a gully or headed up a hill.

They made it to Jake's cabin in four times the amount of time that it normally would have taken. When he propped the structure against the fireplace, she was amazed at how well it belonged. In fact, it appeared as though it had been made for the rocked wall and window light that brought out the winding grooves.

Nellie looked down at the clean, planked floor, imagining a rug in front of a fire. There would be a pot hung above the flames, and the aroma of stew would fill the air. Yes, the cabin could use a woman's touch.

The silence was interrupted by a noise of scratching and thumping. Jake moved into the adjoining room. In soothing tones, he spoke quietly, and Nellie remembered the fawn. She followed him into the room.

"Seems he likes to move around on his own. I left him in the room by the fire, but guess he wanted to explore. Look, he edged himself in here, using his three good legs."

Nellie peered into the room beyond his kneeling form. Bare of decoration, it was obviously a man's room. Glancing around, she saw the big bed against the wall. This was where he slept. His covers were tossed in a heap, spread out at the foot of the unmade bed. She couldn't push away the notion of Jake lying sprawled in the middle. Flushing slightly, she returned her attention to the fawn.

The baby deer lay still, allowing Jake to stroke its neck. On seeing Nellie, the fawn turned big, brown eyes, as if welcoming another gentle touch. She couldn't believe how tame the creature seemed to be.

"This is a little buck. Next spring he'll have short stubs here." He pointed to places behind the ears where antlers would appear.

Judging by the brilliant white spots on the deer's auburn coat, the fawn was less than a month old. Nellie found it difficult to imagine the deer becoming a full-grown buck with a spreading rack of antlers.

Crouching down near Jake, she tentatively reached forward, feeling the animal's smooth coat under her fingertips. She was surprised when she felt the fawn's cool nose touch her arm. The gesture served as a greeting of sorts.

"Sometimes nature gives us gifts," she spoke softly. "The presents aren't wrapped in packages and tied with ribbon." Smiling, she added, "This one here is wrapped in spots."

Jake chuckled. Almost as if he sensed the meaning in her words, the deer rested his head on Jake's upper thigh.

Nellie held her breath. She gazed in wonderment at the scene before her.

Suddenly, another image came to her mind. Her mother sat gently rocking little Mary Ann in her arms as she sang soothingly, *Hush little baby, don't you cry. Mother's going to sing you a lullaby...* As small infants, Nellie and her siblings were eased into a peaceful sleep with the melody in their ears.

Jake's profile resembled that of a father comforting a child. Feeling secure in his presence, the deer was allowing him the contact that only an infant gave to a mother.

Remembering the rusted, metal fangs that had caught the deer in its mouth, Nellie realized that Jake must have descended on the scene like an angel. It was no wonder that he had earned the fawn's trust.

Chapter Eleven

In the weeks that followed, Nellie didn't see Jake very often. Working in the garden filled her days. The vegetables became ripe, one after another. Harvesting became a pattern of snapping green beans, uprooting potatoes, and shucking corn. This year, Rebecca was eight, and despite her petite size, she was quick in deftly gathering up the crop in her over-sized apron pockets.

The Morgans hadn't needed to call on George or Jake this year. Both were doing their own harvesting in their smaller gardens. Nellie's thoughts of Jake were pushed to the back of her mind as she focused on the task of helping her mother prepare for canning.

On Sunday, when the Morgans took a day of rest from the fields, Nellie decided to make a visit that she had been putting off for some time.

Not wishing to appear in any way out of the ordinary, she donned a simple beige cotton dress. In after thought, she picked up the straw hat that she wore when working in the fields. She pulled it snugly over her braids. There, perfect!

With confidence, she saddled Breeze. Once on the gelding, she tugged the reigns in the direction of Jake's cabin. As Nellie rode along, she studied conversation topics that would be of interest to him. There was her father's talk of digging a deeper cellar for the potatoes and John's recently acquired raccoon. The visit would seem like she had come to share the family's news.

When the cabin's tall A-framed roof came into view above the rising hill, she suddenly felt a nervous case of jitters. Sitting up straighter in the saddle, she pulled on the reigns, slowing the horse to a pause.

She stiffened at the sound of laughter. The distance disguised the speakers, but the feminine tones were undeniably familiar.

Abruptly, she jerked the reigns, urging Breeze into the cover of the trees by their side. Dismounting, she led the horse down a bluff where the gelding would not be seen.

Thankful that she had worn beige, the color blended well with the leaves. Nellie crouched low, creeping cautiously forward. Kneeling to the ground, she lay flat on her stomach. Raising only her head, she could take in the scene that would pass before her.

Fortunately, her wait wasn't long. Ten minutes passed. Soon she heard a horse's steady steps, followed by the creaking wheels of what sounded much like a buggy, rustling the leaves.

Although the open buggy passed quickly and was driven by a gentleman that Nellie did not recognize, she could not mistake Mrs. Hallie's overly endowed bosom and her daughter sitting at her side.

Feeling a wave of bitter disappointment, Nellie's shoulders slumped. She pressed her cheek into the crook of her elbow. Studying the broken twigs jutting out from beneath the leaves at her chin, she acknowledged that her life was really not much different from the tiny, torn tree branches.

How could she have been so blind? It was obvious that nothing had changed between Elizabeth and Jake. They were merely getting ready to set up their new home. No doubt her friend was planning a place for lace doilies, and deciding where she would set flower print, porcelain china.

Nellie hugged her arms to her body, suddenly feeling cold. She didn't want to think about the girl's feminine clutter in Jake's home. With a sigh, she got to her feet, and headed back to untie Breeze. This time, she encouraged the horse to follow the river in the direction they had come. There would be no visit today.

The days seemed to drag by much slower after Nellie discovered that Elizabeth May was visiting Jake at his home in the woods.

Tightening the knot on her laced boot with a final jerk, she stood abruptly, dismissing the picture of Jake and Elizabeth making their home together. With a sniff, she straightened the front of her dress. Why should she care if Jake chose Elizabeth as his wife? Any man who made such an unlikely match was certainly not very sensible. And Nellie considered herself far better off without a man who chose frills over practicality.

Placing a lightweight coat over her shoulders, she headed out to the barn where her father and John were hitching a flat bed to the mule. They were preparing for the coming winter and would be hauling in some firewood that had been cut the day before.

It was early October, and the trees were decked out in their fall colors. Despite the warm tones of orange and yellow, Nellie felt a sudden chill as they rode along the roadbed that had been cut into the woods.

She was throwing pine kindling into the corner of the flat bed when she heard footsteps break the leaves. She jumped, startled, only to feel a cold, damp nose nuzzling her side. Looking down quickly, she laughed softly. The creature standing at her side could only be Jake's rescued fawn. Of course, he had lost his spots and had acquired a new gray coat. Looking at the tall deer, Nellie saw that he was no longer a fawn.

"Hey, where'd he come from?" John asked. He dropped the pine logs on the ground that he'd been lifting, kneeling beside the deer.

"Nellie, he doesn't look the same. How'd he get here?" Looking over his shoulder, John called to his father, "Come here, Pa. Look who's here."

"Well, looks like we've got some company."

Joseph looked closely at the deer and continued, "Don't think I've ever had this kind of visit before." He chuckled, reaching out a rough hand to gently stroke the animal's neck.

"He sure is friendly," Nellie commented.

"Yes, he is. But that's because he knows his friends." A deep voice spoke matter-of-factly, a mere distance away. It was Jake!

"Hey there, son. Didn't hear you walk up. That deer must be teaching you something." Joseph chuckled.

While her father and Jake talked, Nellie couldn't help thinking that Jake's words held a double meaning. She felt as though he was making some kind of statement meant for her alone when he had commented that the deer knew his friends. It had been well over a month since she had last spoken to him.

When Jake stayed to help them with the timber, she didn't speak unless spoken to. Jake seemed to sense her indifference and didn't try to draw her out.

This continued throughout the day, and when the last load had been hauled to the barn and stacked, Jake took his leave. Nellie's mother encouraged him to stay for supper, but he thanked her kindly, saying that he had to get back with Bucky. This was the name he had chosen for the small deer.

Glancing out the window at his retreating form, she couldn't help feeling a touch of guilt for her dismissing front. Her shoulders slumped. Neither Jake nor Elizabeth May had ever treated her unkindly, yet she had brushed away the only two friends that she had ever made. This was all due to plain old jealousy.

Chapter Twelve

Snow fell early that year in the fall of 1861. It was mid-November, and Nellie and her brother were out checking their traps. She firmly held a squirming rabbit by its hind legs as John reset the box trap.

"I thinks this one's too small," she commented.

Nellie wouldn't admit it, but she was reluctant to place the small animal in the pouch with the others. Its early end only reminded her of Bucky. Although she loved the taste of venison, it was nearly impossible to eat deer since she had become acquainted with Bucky. Looking at the small rabbit with its floppy ears, she suddenly sensed the terror that the animal must be feeling.

"I'm letting it go," she said.

Opening her hand, the rabbit plunked to the ground. Startled from the unexpected release, it was a moment before the small bundle of fur propelled itself into flight.

"Why'd you do that for?" John demanded. "It was big enough. Pa's sure goin' to be ill with you."

This had been their last trap, and as they turned to walk back home, John mumbled something under his breath about Nellie not getting any food, cause she'd "let' em get away".

White flakes were falling steadily, and they were at a valley near the river where Jake's cabin sat on the bluff to their left.

"Let's go by and see how Jake's making out," she

suggested. She tugged on her brother's arm when he was reluctant to fall into step. She knew that seeing Bucky would get his mind off the rabbit.

With a fist, Nellie beat heavily on Jake's door and was disappointed when he did not answer. Perhaps he wasn't at home. Of course, it wasn't likely that he would be out in this weather. Maybe he was ignoring her. After all, she hadn't been too friendly the last time they had been together.

"Jake, are you there?" her brother called out.

When the door did not open, John ran to the front of the house that looked over the river. Standing on the porch, he could peer through the tall windows into the big room. Nellie sighed. Jake didn't have anything against her brother.

She became worried when John continued to call out. This could only mean that he had gone out. Suddenly, Uncle Bill came to her mind. Was it possible that he had returned? He had said that he would stop in on his way north. Perhaps he had come and prompted Jake to join the fight with him!

"Nellie! Come quick!" John called, pulling Nellie from her thoughts.

Quickly, she rounded the corner of the house, just as she saw her brother's bottom disappearing over the windowsill.

"Wait a minute," she called. "Wait for me!"

John poked his head out of the window, speaking to her urgently. "It's Jake. I think something's wrong!"

"Ouch!" She rubbed the place on her forehead that had hit the top of the window's frame. Nearly falling down on the bare floor, she ran into the adjoining room where her brother had disappeared.

She gasped. Jake was curled tightly like a ball. The navy and burgundy plaid quilt lay neglected in a heap on the floor. The frigid air was numbing. Alarmed, she could see her breath forming a warm cloud.

Quickly, she knelt beside Jake's stiffened form. Easing her body next to his, she placed an arm protectively around his shoulders.

"Come here, John. Get on his other side and hug up. He's really cold and we need to get him warm."

Her brother looked uncomfortable at the prospect of nestling against another male, yet he scampered onto the bed at Nellie's urging.

"Quick. Do as I say. He'll die if he doesn't warm up soon."

Jake groaned. Nellie had never heard a more welcome sound.

"Shhh...," she whispered. "You're going to be okay."

She cradled him to her breast as a mother would a child, pressing her lips above his pallid brow. Holding him tightly, she was thankful that she and John had stopped by at a timely hour.

When the quilt covering the three of them was insulated with warmth, she nudged her brother.

"John, could you build a fire in the big room? There's kindling by the porch."

It was no time before Nellie heard the sound of fire taking spark, and detected the aroma of burning wood. She sighed. A warm fire was something she would never take for granted again.

Easing away from Jake, the bed creaked when she stood. Nestling the warm quilt beneath his chin, she went in search of food. It was no telling when he had last eaten.

Fortunately, the shelves were not bare. She recognized the blue glass jars that her mother used in canning. With a smile, Nellie remembered placing the ripened, red tomatoes and green beans in the very same jars. She hummed softly while scooping the vegetables into a pot for soup.

Placing the cast iron pot on a hook over the fire, it was not long before the vegetables were beginning to simmer. Not wishing to have the soup too hot, she caught the wire handle with a poker that was propped against the rocked wall.

She blew lightly into the warm mug cradled in her palms. She had placed a cloth under its bottom to protect her skin against burning. It was about ready.

"John!" she called.

When he didn't answer right away, she called again.

"Coming!" he answered from outside.

John hopped up onto the porch, and Nellie could see that he wasn't alone. Bucky was trailing at his heels and landed on the plank floor with a bounding leap.

"Look, Bucky still lives here. He caught me taking some kindling from the shed." He grinned, reaching down to pat the deer on the back.

"He's like a dog, ain't he?" John pointed to the deer that was pressing his nose into Nellie's dress for a sniff.

"Yes, he's a pet. But I'd say he's much bigger than a dog."

Placing her hand on John's shoulder, she asked, "Can you help me prop Jake up against the bed's head board so that I can get some soup in him? He needs to eat."

"How's he goin' to eat, Nellie? He looked nearly dead to me."

She was startled by her brother's blunt remark. At fourteen now, he was more talkative than he used to be, and often said exactly what came to mind.

Pushing him along, she replied, "No, he's going to be all right, but we'll have to force feed him."

"What's that?" John interrupted.

"It just means that we'll have to practically pour soup down his throat until he catches on and swallows."

John was about to ask another question, but he became quiet when they had reached Jake. He was lying in the same position that she'd left him.

"You get on that side," she pointed.

Even with the two of them working together, Jake's solid weight would barely budge. Coming up with another tactic, Nellie climbed onto the bed, standing with one foot placed on either side of Jake's head.

Using the wall as a brace, she edged down so that his head could be lifted and laid in her lap. Hooking her elbows beneath his forearms, she hauled Jake's upper body against her chest. She grimaced. His frame had pinned her to the wall!

"Come closer, John. Give me a hand."

Nellie stretched out her arm, motioning for help. Her brother climbed over Jake's sprawled frame, pulling him by the shoulders while his sister pushed. Finally, she was free. Taking a pillow from where it had been wedged under Jake's body, she placed it beneath his head. Sitting back on her heels, she spoke to John in an almost whisper.

"You think he'd know we're here with all the moving we've been making. Why don't you get on the other side again, and help me hold his head."

Nellie reached for the mug that was sitting on the floor. Making sure that only liquid filled the spoon, she pressed the beans to the side. She didn't want to choke Jake.

Prodding his partially open mouth with the tip of the spoon, she tilted it slightly so that the liquid dripped between his lips. Nothing happened.

More determined to get him to swallow, she spooned a much larger dose into his mouth. This time, she poured the liquid into the opening without using much caution. Jake's shoulders shook slightly as he coughed forcefully. Nellie felt a soft spray on her cheek.

"Ugh!" she drew back.

"He's alive!" her brother nearly yelled.

"Of course he is. He's been resting, that's all."

Jake still hadn't opened his eyes. Taking another spoonful, she tilted the straight handle more slowly. Although Jake didn't seem to be fully conscious, his throat muscles flexed as he swallowed.

Nellie's shoulders dropped in relief. He was going to be okay.

It was getting to be late afternoon, and the falling snow was getting much deeper. Nellie knew that she should send John for help. Her folks would be worried if they didn't return soon and Jake needed her mother's attention.

"John, I think it best that you head out before the weather gets any worse. I can't leave Jake here by himself since he's so

92

sick. Tell Pa and Ma to come as soon as they can. I'll see that the place here is warm, and keep feeding him to build back his strength. He's in a deep sleep and not likely to wake up."

"Okay," John nodded.

After her brother left, only the crackling fire broke the silence. Sitting by the hearth, Nellie hugged her knees close to her chest. It was hard to imagine strong, virile Jake Hunter lying helpless in the other room. She peered at his sleeping form through the doorway. From a distance, he only appeared to be resting.

Walking quietly to stand by his side, Nellie did something that she would have never done in any other circumstance. Kneeling over his face, cushioned against the pillow, she lightly kissed his cheek. It was much warmer than it had been earlier.

Feeling self-conscious, she pulled away. Relieved that there was no indication that he'd felt her touch, she took another step. Knowing that he would not awaken for some time, she gained the courage to join him beneath the quilt. She was only getting close to keep the chill off of them both, she decided. Placing an arm around his waist, she sighed, snuggling close.

Chapter Thirteen

Nellie wasn't aware of falling asleep. She only knew that Jake was very sick and was calling her name in a hoarse voice. Where was he? Everything was so dark. She reached her hand into the blackness, beckoning him. *I'm here, Jake. Everything's going to be okay.* He was quiet. Although she could not see him, she knew that he had understood.

Feeling a shift in the cradle that held her, she became alert. Unconscious of her surroundings, Nellie felt that she was being observed. Startled, she hesitated in opening her eyes. Afraid to move, she peeked out. Instantly, she could feel Jake's dark brown eyes on her face. Caught off-guard, she tried to move away from the scrutinizing source. Nellie's movements were halted. A strong arm held her close.

"Well, look who's here," a voice spoke huskily in her ear. "Looks like I've died and gone to heaven," Jake chuckled softly.

Awkwardly aware of how suggestive her presence must seem to him, Nellie stammered, "Oh, you're awake. You've been right sick, and if this is heaven, you look a bit under the weather."

She struggled to move away but was held firmly.

"I don't think being under the weather is so bad, if it means that I'm not in it alone." He grinned, affectionately brushing his nose against hers.

"Oh, you," she scolded in mock disapproval, swatting his upper arm.

Jake ducked his head.

Absent-minded, she placed her hand on the arm that circled her waist. She took a quick intake of breath when warm, hair-roughened skin brushed her fingertips. Not wishing to draw attention, Nellie allowed her hand to rest where she had let it fall.

"How long have you been awake?" she asked.

"Well, let me see," he paused, and amusement danced in his eyes. "I think I must have been in a deep sleep when I dreamed that I was being tied up to the headboard. Funny, but it seemed to have a cushioned back and your voice!" His eyes grew big, taking on a look of incredibility.

Nellie was stunned.

"What? Are you saying that you were awake when I thought you were practically dead to the world?" she exclaimed, irritated.

Seeing that Nellie didn't welcome his teasing, he apologized.

"Come on now, Nell. You know I didn't mean anything by it. I was pretty much out of my head when I realized that I wasn't alone. I only remember hearing voices, and someone trying to drown me in soup." He grinned.

Sighing, she lay still, closing her eyes. She felt like such a fool.

He murmured against her ear, "Nell, I'm sorry."

She felt warm breath brush her forehead when he leaned down to touch his lips lightly to her temples. He continued dropping soft kisses on her brow. When his lips followed a path around her closed eyes in the direction of her mouth, she opened her eyes to meet his.

He murmured her name huskily before closing the few inches between them. His mouth was warm, capturing their breaths together. Pulling her tightly to his frame, Jake nestled his head against her neck.

"Oh, Nell. You don't know how long I've wanted to do that."

Suddenly, she became aware of his burning skin that had nothing to do with the kiss. Pulling back, she placed her palm on his brow.

"Jake, you're so hot, you're practically on fire!"

"Now, don't you worry. I may be a little warm, but I'm all right."

Throwing off his arm, she scampered off the bed. Her eyes adjusted to the dim light, brightened only by the windows from the adjoining room. Making her way to the fireplace, she stroked the burning coals, adding kindling that John had left on the floor.

Hearing footsteps behind her, Nellie turned to find a barefoot Jake.

"You shouldn't be on this cold floor. You should be in bed."

"I will in a minute. This just feels so good." He spread out his hands, edging closer to the fire.

"Yes, the last thing we want is for you to catch your death," she reprimanded in a motherly tone.

He obediently came to stand at her side. She was unprepared, however, when he reached to enfold her in his arms, pulling her back against his shirtfront.

"Umm... I think this is much warmer than the bed," he spoke into her hair. "With both you and the fire's warmth, I should be getting better in no time."

She was surprised when he placed one cold foot over her warmer one.

"Jake, your feet are like ice!"

He moved closer to the fire, shielding her from the flame's heat. They stood there until Nellie began to grow uncomfortably warm and pulled away.

"Are you hungry?" she asked.

"Yeah, that little bit of soup didn't go far," he grinned.

"Serves you right," she said. Reaching for the pot that still hung above the fire, she was interrupted by Jake's hand.

"Hey, let me get that." He took the poker from her hand, deftly hooking the pot's handle.

They ate in silence, and Nellie looked wistfully at the

snow falling outside the tall windows. She had often imagined this scene. At that moment, everything in her life seemed complete if only she wouldn't wake up tomorrow, and find that it had only been a dream. Sitting before the warm fire with Jake's arm around her shoulders, she knew that this was a memory she'd always cherish.

Suddenly, a knocking sounded on the door. Startled, Nellie jumped away from Jake. It was her parents! And Jake wasn't in bed!

"Nellie! It's your pa and ma! Open up."

Hearing her father's voice, she sprang to the door.

"Came as soon as we could. Your ma thought we should bring some quilts for a pallet," Joseph said.

When her parents entered the cabin they seemed taken back to find Jake standing by the fire. Noting his pallor, her mother quickly advised that he should be in bed.

"John said that you were asleep when he left. Didn't even wake up when you were being fed. You really should take care of yourself now," Martha gently reprimanded.

With a hand on his back, she nudged him towards the adjoining bedroom.

"Yeah," he agreed. "I shouldn't have gotten out of bed. Guess the warm fire was enough to wake up these cold bones." He grinned.

"Hear you didn't have a fire when Nellie and John came in. I know how you like the outdoors, but you don't need to bring the cold inside with you," Joseph said, humorously.

Jake chuckled as he left the room, causing a spell of coughing.

Joseph turned to his daughter.

"It's getting dark outside and I need to be heading back. The drifts are getting worse and the kids are by themselves. You and your ma will be staying here tonight."

Handing her the quilts, he suggested that she make a pallet close to the fire.

Hearing that her husband was getting ready to leave,

Martha came back into the room.

She wiped the back of her hand across her forehead.

"The boy's resting now, but he has a fever." Biting her lip, she turned to her husband, "When you come in the morning, please bring my satchel of herbs. Jake will be needing them."

Looking at her daughter, she continued, "If you and John hadn't stopped by today, there's no telling how Jake would be. He has both of you to thank." She smiled, reaching to lay a hand on Nellie's shoulder.

Morning came, and although Jake's temperature had fallen, he was not yet awake. Martha was getting worried.

"I hope your father comes soon. Until he does, let's try to keep Jake cool. Please fill this mug with snow."

Lacing the boots that nearly reached her knees, Nellie prepared to venture outdoors. As a precaution against the chilling wind, she wrapped a thick, woolen scarf around her head, making sure that only her face was exposed.

Her first step out into the white landscape was almost blinding. Squinting, she paused. When her eyes had adjusted to the brilliance, she stooped to break the layer of ice on top. Teeth chattering, she quickly filled the mug.

Nellie carried the snow to Jake's bedside where Martha stood ready with a dry cloth. Taking the mug, her mother proceeded to dip the cloth into the melting snow. Jake jerked slightly against the cold contact when the moistened cloth touched his fevered forehead.

Smoothing the hair back from his forehead, her mother hummed softly. When the cloth grew warm, she dipped it again. Soothing, the lullaby eased Jake into a relaxed state, and he did not move this time when the cold cloth touched his brow.

"Ma, I'm going out to feed Jake's horse. Pa should be coming soon." Nellie said.

"Okay, dear. Just don't stay out too long. I'll warm something for us to eat."

Nellie stepped into the small shed where Storm was sheltered. Her father had given Jake the horse for his help with the harvest. When the door creaked open, the stallion neighed in welcome. Murmuring a greeting, she reached up to pat his neck.

It was hard to believe that this was the same horse that had once made her feel uneasy. Jake had won his trust. She found a tub of sweet feed in a tiny closet built in the far corner of the building.

Storm stepped expectantly forward when the sound of his morning meal was poured into the trough. Taking an armful of hay, she placed it into another trough. She nodded. That should do him for the day.

Nellie stepped out of the shed in time to see her father riding through the trees.

"Are we glad to see you!" Nellie exclaimed.

"How's Jake this morning?" Joseph asked. "I came as soon as the girls were fed."

Nellie glanced towards the cabin with a frown on her face.

"He was doing better last night when you left. We thought everything was going to be okay, but this morning he's burning with fever. He isn't awake yet, but Ma says the herbs will give him strength."

When they entered the cabin, her mother hurried forward. Motioning for Joseph to bring the saddlebags closer, she reached in for a bottle of dark liquid. With a grimace, Nellie remembered this remedy. It was an herbal blend of catnip and yellow root, laced with peppermint. The latter was used to enhance the taste of the bitter yellow root that would strengthen the body's ability to fight disease.

Adding a small amount of the potion to a mug of snow, her mother soon had a tea warming over the fire. Before the liquid could grow too hot, she spooned a small amount between Jake's lips. He jerked when his taste buds came in contact with the bitter solution. The awful flavor was enough to wake anyone up, Nellie thought, shaking her head.

Following the dosage, the morning passed quickly with Martha periodically giving instructions to have the door fanned for fresh air, or to have the tea heated over the fire. It was mid-day before Jake finally awoke. Nellie jumped up quickly when she heard him speaking to her mother.

She entered the room just as he was propping himself up on his elbows. He paused in his speech, muttering something that she could not decipher. Her mother was busy straightening the covers and looked up when she saw her daughter.

"Well, our sick boy has woken up."

Nellie looked at Jake and could not find the little sick boy image that she had associated with her mother's words. Sheepishly remembering their exchange, she saw only an attractive man whose bare chest was exposed where the quilt lay at his waist. He had been wearing a shirt during the night. She looked away quickly in embarrassment. Seeing the bucket at her mother's feet, Nellie knew that she was giving Jake a light wash.

"Hey son, glad to see you're awake. Wondered how long we should let you sleep," Joseph remarked with a grin as he entered the room.

"From what Mrs. Morgan tells me, I was sleeping like a bear."

"If you'd slept much longer, we would've had to send an army in to wake you up," her father laughed.

Jake joined in, yet his laughter soon turned to a fit of coughing. Nellie's mother shooed her husband from the room.

"Go along, now. The boy needs rest. There'll be time for kidding later."

Nellie left with her father. She didn't feel comfortable under her mother's observant gaze. Afraid that her heart would betray her, she did not want anyone to see her tender concern for Jake.

Martha followed her from the room.

"Jake is going to need someone with him, again, tonight. I'll stay here, and your father will take you home so that you can look after your sisters."

Hugging her daughter, she gestured towards the room where Jake lay.

"He will want to know that you're leaving. Look in on him before you go."

Nellie walked to the bed on tiptoe, almost hoping that he had fallen back to sleep. Hearing a plank creak, his eyes opened. Giving her a warm smile, Jake took her hand. She turned abruptly so that her back faced the open doorway, and her parents could not witness the intimate gesture.

"I've got to go tend the girls now," she said. "I hope you'll rest and get well." She lightly squeezed his hand.

"Wish you weren't going," he spoke softly. "You've been such a big help to me. There's no telling how I'd be if you hadn't stopped by yesterday." Bringing her fingers to his mouth, he kissed her knuckles tenderly.

"As soon as I'm well, I'll ride over. I think there's some things we need to talk about." He looked deeply into her eyes while his fingers traced a pattern in her palm.

Nellie's heart beat quickened. She smiled weakly. Murmuring goodbye, she felt like dancing from the room. Jake could only want to discuss one thing. Gathering the scarf about her face, she pulled the fabric over her eyes, disguising the exuberant joy.

Chapter Fourteen

Nellie waited anxiously for Jake's visit after her mother and father returned home. Her hopes fell when nearly three weeks passed, and he did not come to call.

It was only a few weeks before Christmas, when Nellie was scrubbing the bread dough from her fingers, a knock sounded at the door. She quickly dried her hands when she heard the deep tones of Jake's voice. Brushing back the tendrils escaping her bun, she felt hesitant to make an appearance.

She wondered if he would speak to her in private. What if he had changed his mind since they had last spoken? After all, he had been ill when he had mentioned that they needed to talk.

Still wiping her hands on the dampened cloth, Nellie used the gesture as an excuse for not drawing Jake out when she entered the room. Looking up, she was surprised to find that Jake was not alone. Uncle Bill was standing at his side, gritting his teeth in aggravation. He stamped his booted foot on the floor, speaking harshly.

"No sense in letting those dad-blamed Yankees think they can just walk in and take over! A fellow was telling me how they pulled one over his old aunt. Came right through the door and said they needed a place for the bleeding sick. Heck, wasn't a sick man in the bunch!

Nearly starved the poor soul to death! And it being near Thanksgiving time to boot. Why, she didn't have nary a bite left when they high-tailed it out of there!" his voice rose, angrily.

"I've worked too hard to have them come in and ransack my place. I won't have them thinking they can just walk in and set up house," Jake muttered in frustration.

"And they ain't goin' to!" Bill spat out. "We'll stop them in their tracks when they see the likes of us." He laughed without any real mirth.

Nellie felt as though a heavy stone had replaced her heart. No! She couldn't be hearing right. Jake couldn't be joining the rebels with his uncle, not with Christmas only a few days away!

"We'll be heading out this afternoon. Goin' to meet up with some fellahs outta this side of the woods. We'll give those dang Yanks a run for their lives!"

Feeling Jake's eyes, Nellie looked up to find him watching her. He smiled slowly, closing the few steps between them. He gestured towards the door, and they passed through quietly. The family was too caught up in Bill's plan of action to notice their departure.

After the cabin's door had closed behind them, Nellie stood with her back against the wall. A solemn expression rested on her face, and she tightened her lips grimly.

"Chin up," Jake said softly, lifting her jaw lightly with his fingers.

She smiled weakly, gazing at a point beyond his shoulder.

"I would've come sooner if I'd known I was going away. Bill just dropped in a couple of days ago, and I decided last night that I'd go with him."

"Do you have to go?" she asked distantly.

"Yeah, I do." he returned. "If we don't take a stand, we could lose everything we've worked for."

Nellie frowned. She certainly didn't want the law telling her how to live. In her mind, she saw the busy, crowded streets and houses side by side with tiny yards. This was the place Yankees called home. There were no trees, rivers or fields where vegetables grew. She shuddered, pushing the bleak image away.

"What are you thinking?" he asked.

"That maybe you're right. I'd hate to think that all those

people could come into our woods and change the way we live."

Jake nodded.

"I thought you'd understand. Once we all go up against those Yankees, the fight won't last too long. We'll push them back in no time."

When Nellie didn't speak, Jake pulled her slight frame against his much stronger one. There were many questions that she wanted to ask, but she kept them to herself. Some things were better left unsaid.

He held her protectively, and she relaxed in the shelter of his arms. She sighed. If only they could stay this way forever. There'd be no parting, no war, and no questions.

The door creaked open, causing Nellie to jump. Pulling away from Jake, she clasped her hands nervously behind her back. Fortunately, his Uncle Bill did not see them because he was looking over his shoulder, laughing, as he shared some joke with her father.

Soon the entire family came out and stood huddled against the cold. Nellie shivered. The day was dismal in its gray overtones. Tugging at her memory was a similar day. It had been a very long time ago. She had been about nine.

She felt the raindrops splashing on the toes of her lace-up boots. Pressed close to her father's side, she was wrapped in the heavy folds of his coat. Unfortunately, the woolen fabric did not keep the cold dampness from seeping in.

Her mother was sobbing softly. A dark coffin was lowered into a freshly dug hole that was beginning to fill with water. The sight seemed unreal. Nellie couldn't understand why her grandmother was lying inside the box. It had been the last time that she had seen Grandma Sarah.

Jake's voice broke into her thoughts.

"Nell, take care. I'd like to stay longer, but we're going to meet up with some others, and there's supplies to get at the mill." He embraced her tightly, before reaching to hug her sisters.

Before he could hug Mary Ann, she wrapped her arms around his legs.

"Come see me soon," she exclaimed, unaware of the risk that Jake was undertaking.

Nellie sighed. She envied her little sister's simple understanding of the things around her. With a child's innocence, she was not saddened by Jake's departure. She knew only that he would return. Clapping John on the shoulder, Jake said, "I'd appreciate you checking on Bucky for me. He'd get lonely if there was never anyone around."

Jake and his uncle finished bidding their farewells as they mounted the horses. Turning away, Jake lifted his hat in parting. For a brief instant, Nellie saw the Indian warrior of her daydreams in the set of his broad shoulders and dark hair. This time her brave was heading out on a path of war!

Winter passed like the snowflakes that fell silently outside the Morgan's cabin. There had been no word from Jake. Looking out at the white landscape, Nellie couldn't imagine why people wanted to fight in this kind of weather. She snuggled under the covers, turning her head from the window.

Jake had been gone three months, and Christmas had been different that year. It had been the first time that Nellie hadn't anticipated the coming season. Of course, Christmas had been solemn for everyone.

Many families had watched their men folk assemble companies, join regiments, and hurry to a battle far away. With the absence of husbands and elder sons, household maintenance was left to wives and small children.

Fortunately, Joseph Morgan remained behind with his family. The strain of travel and battle would have been too much for his ailing health. For once, Nellie was thankful that her father was out of harm's way.

But what about Jake? Where was he, now? Was he all right? She hugged her pillow tightly, imagining that she held Jake. "I love you," she whispered, puckering her lips to give the fabric an imaginary kiss.

She pulled back. Love? What did it mean? She loved

her family, the outdoors, and the tasty twang of apple cider. She loved all kinds of little things, but none of them filled her heart like Jake.

Feeling lighter, she pressed her cheek into the warm cloth. She imagined that she felt Jake's skin against her face. His lips would trace a path across her brow, dropping small tender kisses on her closed eyes. She smiled.

"Nellie!"

She jumped, breaking away from her daydreams. Her face flushed in embarrassment. She hoped Rebecca had not witnessed the kiss.

"Nellie, Ma said you'd braid my hair."

Her sister, nearly twelve, was growing up fast. Already, she insisted on colorful ribbons being braided into her hair, and today, she wore the red bow that she had been given for Christmas. "Pretty as a picture," her mother had remarked. Yes, her sister was going to be a very beautiful lady.

Hopping onto the bed, Rebecca bounced lightly. She smoothed her frock over her legs, straightening the bow over her bodice.

"Could you give me one braid instead of two? And I'd like the blue ribbon. It will look pretty with my bow." She patted the material as she spoke.

"All right. Move closer."

Separating her sister's blond hair into three parts, she began to weave the strands together. Over, under, over, under. Intent on her task, she was startled when Jake's name was mentioned.

"What did you say again, Rebecca?"

"Do you ever miss Jake?" her sister asked.

"Why, of course. We all do."

Rebecca spoke quietly this time. "Do you think he's coming back?"

"Well, yes. He has a home here, you know."

Her sister hesitated. "That's not what I mean, Nellie. What if he *can't* come back?"

106

Surprised that Rebecca had voiced the thought that she, herself, would like to have ignored, Nellie hugged the little girl's petite frame. Brushing a tendril from Rebecca's brow, she dropped a kiss on her sister's forehead.

"Shh... Hush now. Don't say that."

"He'll be okay, won't he, Nell?"

Taking her sister's hand, she placed it, palm down, over the little girl's heart.

"You feel that? It's keeping you here. When you go to sleep at night, you always wake up in the morning, don't you?"

Rebecca nodded.

"Jake has one, too, and his is keeping him here. The good Lord keeps our hearts beating, and we forget they're there."

She patted Rebecca's dress front, bringing a smile to the girl's face. Accepting this explanation, her sister reached up to trace the ribbon threaded in her hair.

"Someday, the ribbon will be too short for my hair." Turning, she made a sweeping motion behind her back, indicating the length of her hair. "My hair will be so long that it will touch the floor!"

Nellie had to smile. As she grew older, Rebecca would attract the attention of many young boys. She was thankful that her sister was still a little girl in Jake's eyes. She wouldn't want her own flesh and blood as a rival. Elizabeth May was enough!

It had been quite some time since she had seen her blond friend. She had almost forgotten the buggy that she had seen coming from Jake's home. Why had he never mentioned Elizabeth's visit? Possibly, because she hadn't been around when he could have told her about it. Had he guessed that she was jealous of Elizabeth?

Her shoulders fell. Had Jake really hinted at something more than friendship? Or was she just imagining it? She wondered if his intentions had changed only because he had found her in bed. Looking back at the incident, she felt uncomfortable. Nellie could've pinched herself for being so naive. She was still living in a dream world!

Chapter Fifteen

The cold winter days melted into spring of 1862. A month earlier, Nellie had turned seventeen. There had been no birthday surprise like her sixteenth year; however, her mother had cooked her favorite meal of chicken and dumplings.

It was now May, and her father was loading the wagon that would be taken to the trading post sat up in the field behind Dan's mill.

Joseph's bee logs had been successful this year and the delicious honey had been placed in blue jars lined against the wagon's headboard. Nestled against the round containers, her mother had placed pouches of dried apple rinds. Also, there were two bushels of potatoes from their root cellar.

"Help me up!" Mary Ann demanded. She could only reach the wagon's bed with her hands, and was hopping impatiently.

"Wait a minute," Nellie said, shaking her head. Her little sister was becoming a handful. No longer a baby, she was strong-willed and quick to speak.

Reaching down, she hooked her elbows under Mary's armpits. One, two, three. She pulled up too quickly, throwing herself off-balance. Stumbling backwards, Nellie fell onto her backside, bringing her sister with her.

Mary Ann giggled, throwing small arms around her older sister's neck. Laughing, she kissed Nellie's cheek while wrapping her in a hug.

"I like that! Let's do it again!"

Standing up and brushing off her skirt, Nellie shook her head. "No, that's enough for right now."

"Everyone up?" her father called from his seat on the front.

"Yes," answered a chorus of voices.

"No!" Nellie interrupted. "Just a minute"

John reached down to grab Mary so that Nellie could climb up.

The Morgans were taking this trip along with other neighboring families who were coming to buy and sell their wares.

The journey seemed much shorter than it had with Jake. Nellie found herself caught up in the excitement as her siblings chattered non-stop. Rebecca was describing the colorful ribbons she would buy while John was speaking of trading his traps. He had brought along two rabbit boxes that he had formed with short, wide planks.

"I'm going to trade 'em for a 'coon hat," he said. The furry hats featuring a dangling tail were becoming popular. Nellie thought that they looked rather silly. She couldn't imagine Jake wearing one!

"Hey there, Joseph!" an elderly man called out. They slowed to a halt behind a row of wagons lining the field. Her father jumped to the ground, giving the short, bent man a hearty pat on the back.

"Hey there, Ed! How've you been?"

"Oh, I'm hanging in there. These legs ain't what they used to be." The old man grinned, patting the worn, faded material covering his knees.

Nellie hopped down, smoothing the folds of her dress. The rose gingham, accenting her peach-ivory skin tone, had become a favorite.

She glanced around, ready to stretch her legs.

"Ma, Nellie will look after me." Rebecca stamped her foot. "Please, can I? I'll be good. I promise."

"All right," her mother answered.

"Nellie, please take Rebecca with you, and make sure you're back in an hour. We'll be getting ready for the big picnic at noon."

Hopping lightly, Nellie felt like a little girl again. How she loved this time of year! She eyed the tables being set up for food. There would be ham sandwiches, chunky potato salad, and thick crusted apple cobbler. Each family contributed to the feast, and the tables nearly overflowed!

"Look! Ribbons!"

Excited, Rebecca skipped ahead. Thin woven strips of red, blue and yellow braided ribbons blew in the breeze. Soft, plump pillows formed into rolls, tied at both ends, were lying on the wagon's bed. The cushions were protected from the bed's rough surface by a lace beige tablecloth. Nellie found the fancy trimmings out of place in the open field.

"Why hello, Nellie!" The lilting voice caused her to turn abruptly. Oh no, not Elizabeth May! Not here.

"Uh, hello." She forced herself to meet Elizabeth's gaze.

"My, it's been a long time. But I guess you've had quite a lot to keep you busy this past winter."

When Nellie didn't answer, she continued cheerfully, "Why, I heard that you were in the right place, at the right time on one snowy day."

Nellie's breath caught. Elizabeth paused.

"Must have been real cozy looking after Jake when he needed a helping hand. He says that you may have saved his life," she murmured sweetly.

Nellie's heart sank. She clenched her hands. Eyes burning, she held back tears that threatened to fall. No, it couldn't be true! Or was it? Had Jake just been playing with her feelings? How else could Elizabeth May have known about that day? Hurt, she had been betrayed.

Feeling a tug on her skirt, Nellie reached to touch Rebecca's hand.

"Look Nellie, isn't it pretty?"

110

Rebecca held a pale pink bow with strands of baby blue ribbon tied to its center.

"Yes, it's pretty. But do you have anything to match those colors? I believe that particular bow looks a bit young for you."

Nellie saw the crestfallen expression on her sister's face and was immediately sorry. Placing an arm around Rebecca's shoulders, she gestured towards a deeper shade of blue, lined with red interfacing.

"Look at this one." Pointing to the soft, deeper blue she continued, "This one will go with your eyes."

She held the bow against her sister's face, and murmured, "Yes. It's perfect."

Rebecca smiled. "Okay. I'll take it."

Elizabeth May reached beneath the wagon, taking out a thin paper that Nellie had never seen. She wrapped the bow in the pale paper, and tied the small package with a string.

"This is the way gifts are wrapped when we buy them in town. Of course, they use ribbon in pretty colors for the string."

Shrugging her shoulders, she frowned, gesturing towards the coarse string as she spoke, "We'll have to make do with this for now."

Wearing a haughty smile, she presented the package to Rebecca.

"Nellie, we really should get together for the picnic. There's a lot of catching up we need to do." Elizabeth placed her hand on Nellie's arm as she spoke. Nellie had to fight the urge to brush it aside.

She spoke doubtfully, "Well, if there's time. I'll be helping the women with the food. There's a lot to do."

"There's always a lot of work," Elizabeth chided. "You just have to make time for the things that you really want to do."

Talking to Elizabeth May was the one thing that she really *didn't* want to do. Frankly, she had no intention of fitting the blond girl into her day.

As they walked away, Rebecca chattered. She couldn't wait to see how the bow would match her blue dress. Did she look grown-up wearing the bow? Could Nellie put it in her hair? She wanted to wear it now.

Pausing, Nellie held up her sister's thick blond braid. She tied the bow at the braid's end.

"How does it look?" Rebecca insisted. "Is it too big for my hair?"

"It looks fine," Nellie reassured.

On their return, she kept very busy helping her mother and the other ladies with the picnic preparations. Looking for any excuse to stay busy, she offered to help serve. There were always pitchers to pour, children who needed help with their plates, and scraps to be taken away.

A cluster of men had gathered at the back of one wagon, and worried voices carried over the breeze. They were discussing the Union's invasion of Tennessee. In February, the Yankees had defeated the Confederates at Fort Henry. Their leader, General Grant, had even moved up the Tennessee River, seizing the railroads. They feared the enemy was getting too close for comfort.

Anxious, Nellie wondered if Jake's family was out of harm's way. They lived in Tennessee. She shuddered. What about Jake and his Uncle Bill? Where were they? It was an awful feeling to know that something could have already happened.

She tried to push the bleak thought aside, playing with the food on her plate. Suddenly, she wasn't hungry. But she pretended to eat when she noticed Elizabeth from the corner of her eye. The girl sat primly with her mother, dressed like a doll that should have been sitting somewhere on a shelf. She wasn't dressed for work or the outdoors.

Nellie sighed. What did Jake see in her? Couldn't he tell that life with Elizabeth would be like a story from a book? The kind of story where everything was make-believe. There would be no fairy tale ending for the two of them. The corner of Nellie's lips rose in a smile that did not reach her eyes.

When the picnic was over, Nellie was happy to find that

the things they had brought to the field had quickly been traded. They had only been there a short time before their wagon was emptied. Because of the looming threat of invasion, women were gathering up food supplies. It was very likely that many of the men folk would be away when it came time to work the summer crop.

The Morgans would have stayed longer, but little Mary Ann began to complain of a tummy ache. For once, Nellie was thankful to get away. Quiet and withdrawn, she stared bleakly at the passing countryside as the wagon bumped over ruts in the dirt road. How could Jake have been so disloyal? Did she really know him? Shaken and torn by conflicting emotions, she would not enter that dream world again. Little Nellie had grown up.

Chapter Sixteen

Summer came and Nellie went through the usual motions of helping her family with the planting, weeding, and harvesting. The labor was much easier this year with three Morgan children in the field.

The warm weather also presented an ideal setting for the raging battles between the Rebels and the Yankees. The war hadn't reached a quick end like Jake had predicted. The South was out-numbered, she'd heard.

Worried, Nellie wondered if Jake was okay. Where could he be? She looked beyond the trees bordering the field. There seemed to be nothing but forest. It was hard to imagine a place in the woods where there was neither peace nor quiet, only gunfire, and hundreds of men rushing towards one another. It was a much bigger event than it had seemed when Uncle Bill and Jake were talking about it.

A lot had changed since that time. Nellie felt detached when she thought of Jake. It was an odd feeling, almost as if he was a stranger again, except she had known him well enough to be hurt. She couldn't blame him really. After all, she had been the one living in a dream world of her own making. He hadn't made a commitment or broken a promise. She had misunderstood him. That was all.

Reaching up, she pushed a stray tendril into her bun. She no longer wore her hair in braids. Frowning, she knew that when Jake had left, he had taken the little girl in her, with him. He had been gone nearly a year now, and in that time, Nellie had grown up.

Turning aside from her idle pondering, she hung the family's clothes to dry on the string extending between two posts in the yard. The season was going to be what people called an Indian Summer. It was only three weeks into the month of September, and the heat felt like July or August. Nellie brushed the perspiration from her forehead with a small cloth from her pocket.

Frowning, she looked up curiously at the sound of hooves. They weren't expecting company. Who could it be?

A wagon pulled into the yard driven by a gaunt, unshaven man. Tufts of hair stuck through the holes in his battered hat. His loose garments were held together with bits of rope for a belt. On closer inspection, the clothes turned out to be that of a dusty, gray uniform. Why, the man was a soldier! But he looked like a scarecrow!

Nellie's heart raced. Why was he here? There was a war going on. Was there trouble?

Her father came out to greet the visitor. Even though she strained to hear their words, she could not understand what was being said. The man gestured towards the wagon's bed, causing Joseph to step back when he peered over its side. He looked up, startled, and called for his wife.

Oh no! Something was wrong. She could sense it. Nellie's mother hurried out quickly with Laura and Mary Ann following close behind. When Martha reached the wagon, she pressed her hand over her mouth, shaking her head in disbelief. She motioned for the girls to stay back.

Nellie hurried quickly to her mother. She caught her breath when she looked over the wagon's side and saw the person lying on the floor. Looking ragged and torn in his dusty gray uniform, the soldier tried to smile.

"How've you been, Nell?" He greeted in a tired, husky voice that sounded much older than the last time she had heard him speak.

It was Jake! But he looked so much older, almost as though he had aged quite a few years in the short year that he had been away.

"Oh, okay," she replied distantly.

She looked away from the large, darkened stain that covered his thigh. His uniform was soiled and bloodied in spots. He had been wounded, and there were no shoes on his feet. They were cut, bruised, and appeared as if they had been bare for a long time.

Rebecca and John had joined the throng of people around the wagon.

"Now, stand back," her mother told them gently. "We're going to get Jake inside the cabin where he can rest better."

Gesturing towards John, she said with maternal authority, "Come help your father and please be careful. Be easy with his legs."

Leading the way into the cabin while Rebecca held the door, Martha smiled over her shoulder.

"You can have your old room again. It will be like old times."

Nellie looked away. Things would never be like they had once been. She watched her father and brother supporting Jake into the cabin. He had lost weight and dark hair fell past his shoulders. His jaw line appeared more chiseled and his eyes were shadowed.

"Nellie, could you get a fire going? I'm going to need hot water to clean Jake's cuts."

Determined to lift the cloud that his arrival had caused, Jake chuckled softly, "It has been a long time since I've had a good washing. Just don't mind the dirt."

"Oh, it's to be expected," her mother nodded. "It will wash off and you'll look more like yourself again." She smiled, brushing a lock of hair away from his face.

Nellie walked through the breezeway to start a fire so the water could be warmed. She sat back on her heels, trying to absorb the day's events. Jake had come home! Despite her earlier confidence, she didn't feel so grown up now.

Soon, a fire crackled, adding to the day's warmth. Testing the water, Nellie quickly dipped her finger beneath the surface. "Ouch!" She waved her hand. It would have to cool a few minutes so that it wouldn't scorch Jake's skin.

Martha had drawn a curtain across the entrance to Jake's room, causing Nellie to pause outside the doorway.

"Ma, the water's ready," she called.

"Okay, dear. Could you bring me a pail of spring water? Have your brother bring in the hot water."

"Be right back," Nellie answered.

When she returned, Jake's torn, blood-stained uniform was lying in a crumpled bundle on the floor. She blushed, imagining his tan, sinewy torso lying against the blankets. Shaking her head, she chided herself for thinking too much.

Setting the bucket outside the curtain, she called, "The spring water's here."

"Thank you, dear."

Nellie turned away, reluctant to leave. Not wanting to be found hovering by Jake's door, she joined her father in the family room.

Sighting his daughter, he shook his head when he spoke.

"The war's not as far away as I'd thought. Believe Jake brought a little bit of it back with him. Seems more real now."

Nellie nodded.

"Makes you wonder just how many boys won't be coming home. Their ma's and pa's will never see them again. Good thing John is still young. Don't know how I'd feel if it was my boy in that other room." His voice trailed off, tears moistening his eyes.

Chapter Seventeen

In the following days Jake slept much of the time. When he felt well, Joseph helped him into the family room. Nellie's mother propped pillows behind his back so that he sat in comfort near the stove. He walked with a limp and used Joseph's shoulder for support.

His left leg had been badly torn by a bullet. Her mother feared that gangrene would set in if it were not cleaned regularly. Nellie learned that gangrene meant that the wound could get infected and the flesh around it would die. Jake could very well lose his leg.

Grimacing, Jake recalled the men who had lost limbs on the battlefield to a doctor's sharp blade. It was believed that the body would heal after the infection was hacked away. With vehemence, he said that he'd rather die before having his vital parts sawed away. He wasn't a tree, and he didn't intend to be a stump!

Shivering, Nellie recalled his vivid description of the battlefield on the day he'd been shot. She didn't have to shut her eyes to visualize the sunken road strewn with bodies near a place called Antietam Creek. They had been fighting in a cornfield on enemy soil.

A cornfield of all places! The picture didn't quite fit her image of the North. Thousands had died on both sides, and more lives had been lost in one day than in all the other battles combined.

One of those men had been Jake's Uncle Bill. Dead. It was hard to imagine the bold talking man gone. He had seemed so full of life when he had ridden away on that dreary, cold day nearly a year ago. His lively gestures had contrasted sharply with the still, gray air around him.

She felt a light touch on her shoulder and looked around. Her mother spoke softly, "Dear, Jake's been asking about you this morning. I think he'd like to talk to you. Won't you step in to see him?"

Nodding, Nellie murmured, "Okay".

When she entered the room, Jake was lying with his back to the door. Thinking that he may be asleep, she turned to leave.

"Don't go," he spoke.

"Oh, I didn't want to disturb you," she said awkwardly.

"You've been keeping your distance from me. I know I look pretty awful, but it's not contagious," he kidded dryly. "You doing okay?"

Shrugging her shoulders, she couldn't meet his eyes when she answered.

"Uh, yeah." She paused, and continued, "I'm just getting used to you being here again. A lot of time has passed. Things have changed."

He lifted an eyebrow. "What's changed?"

Feeling uncomfortable, she looked down at the floor. No, she wouldn't shy away from his questions.

Meeting his eyes, she replied, "We've changed. I'm not the little girl that you left behind, and you've experienced more in the past year than a person normally does in a lifetime."

"Little girl," he chuckled, "so that's how you saw yourself. Could have fooled me." His voice was almost a murmur.

Nellie peered at him now, trying to find the young man that he used to be. The war had torn him on the inside in a way that was not obvious like the damage on his skin.

"Come here. Sit by the bed." He struggled to prop himself up.

Hesitating, she slowly sat down on the bed's edge.

119

Against her back, she could feel the warmth that radiated from his frame. No, some things had not changed. She suppressed a sigh, her shoulders straight.

She nearly jumped when his roughened hand touched her arm.

"Nellie, it's been too long. I wanted to be back here so bad. So many things make sense now that I didn't understand when I left. You know, in the beginning, a war with the North seemed the only way to go. It was either lose our freedom to Yankee rule or fight back so they would leave us alone."

He chuckled without humor, looking off into the distance.

"But it was not as easy as we thought. We marched for days on end 'til the shoes fell off our feet. Tired and hungry, we ate mostly corn and apples, sometimes nothing at all. Looking back, I can see now why those Yankees took our food. They must have been hungry, too. Still, that doesn't excuse them. If it weren't for them, there wouldn't have been any war, and Uncle Bill would not be dead." He sighed, his voice becoming low.

"Nell, it was so awful. I shut my eyes, but I can still see the bodies falling like rain. The bullets sounding like thunder. Couldn't hear anything. Couldn't think straight. So much going on at once. Bumping into one another. Stumbling over bodies. Just had to keep moving to dodge the bullets." He squeezed his eyes shut, opening them slowly.

Tracing a rough path on the inside of her wrist, he spoke hoarsely, "There were days when you were all I could think about, Nell. Didn't know if I would ever see you again. Too much left unsaid. And so much we should've done." He sighed.

Nellie stiffened. He paused.

"What's wrong? Something's bothering you, isn't it?"

Breathing deeply, she spoke hesitantly, "Like I said before, people change. And like you, I see things a bit differently than I did at first. When I first saw you in the woods two years ago, it was like you had walked right out of my daydreams." She looked at him closely. "I was like that, then. Always had my head in the clouds. Always imagining things."

Seeing his questioning look, she continued, "You see, I wanted life to be like a fairy tale. One where a pretty girl meets a handsome man and they both live happily ever after."

She paused, gazing down at her clasped fingers. "Except there was one big problem. There was no handsome man in my life. There was only me. And when you came along that day in the woods, you were the brave warrior who had come to rescue me from my loneliness." Uncomfortable, she could feel a flush rising in her face.

"...So you see, after a while, I confused you with the hero that I wanted you to be, and the person that you really are."

A puzzled look crossed his face, and he teased, "You mean I'm really *not* your handsome warrior?"

Nellie shrugged. "That's not what I mean."

She swallowed. "Remember when you were sick last winter?"

He nodded, and she shifted nervously.

"Well, I read too much into what you told me that night. I thought our relationship had changed, that I was more than just a friend. When you went off to fight, it was like you had become the warrior of my daydreams." Her voice trailed off.

"It can be possible," he spoke softly.

Surprised, Nellie turned to face him. Did she hear him right?

"I d-don't understand," she stammered.

"It's simple. I'll be the brave you want me to be, and you'll be the lady who gives me a reason to become her hero."

Jake gently brushed his fingers across her cheek. He grinned and she couldn't help smiling in return.

There were still the nagging questions in her mind. Nellie wasn't forgetting Elizabeth May. What did the girl mean to him? Now was the time to ask. Before their silence grew awkward, she spoke.

"Jake, I think there are some things that we should talk about." Picking at a loose thread on her dress, she continued, "How does Elizabeth May fit into your life?"

Surprised, he answered, "She's just a friend."

"But it hasn't been too long ago that you admitted your attraction to her. You told me all about it, remember?"

Brushing her question aside with a hand in the air, he replied, "Oh, that didn't last long. Yes, in the beginning, I was curious. She was a pretty girl who made it known that she found me attractive. I liked that. But after a while, she was throwing all kinds of hints, and I started to back away. I began to see her in a different light. You know, we could never talk the way that you and I do. Or at least, when I did talk, I don't think she was really listening, and we weren't interested in the same things." He paused, squeezing her hand,

"...And then there was you, the girl I couldn't stop thinking about. Only you kept your distance and treated me like a brother." He chuckled.

"Nellie, I finally realized that you cared when you helped nurse me back to health. Despite my illness, I felt better in here," he tapped his chest, "than I've ever felt in my life. Afterwards, I didn't come to visit you right away because I was trying to get up the nerve to ask for your hand." He paused, looking away.

"What if you had refused, or what would your pa think about me going sweet on you right after I'd been sick? I wanted the time to be right, Nell, " he said gently.

"And then the next thing I knew, Bill came by. I didn't want to go with him at first, but I couldn't risk the Yankees taking away everything that I had to offer a lady."

Nellie had been holding her breath. He did want to marry her! But then she remembered Elizabeth's last comment. They had been together before he went off to fight.

"Did you see Elizabeth after you were sick?" she asked.

"Yes, but only by accident. Some fellows were meeting up near the mill, and we had to pass her house on the way through. She and her mother came out to watch, not knowing that I'd be with them. When I stopped to say 'hello' Mrs. Hallie began to talk." He chuckled. "You know how long that can take."

"What did you tell Elizabeth May?" she inquired.

"Oh, not much. I mentioned my being sick, and you taking care of me." He grinned. "I don't think that went over too well."

"Oh," Nellie murmured.

He leaned close, pulling her into his arms.

"Ouch!"

She sensed his sudden discomfort, and eased away.

"No, don't go. Stay close." He held her tightly for a moment, whispering in her hair, "I'm so happy to be able to hold you again."

Pointing to a worn satchel on the floor, he asked that she hand it to him. Digging into the parcel, he brought out a small, framed photograph. He placed it in her hand, commenting, "I want you to keep this always, and every time you look at it, know that I was thinking of you when the picture was being taken."

Nellie looked down at the dark, attractive soldier wearing the new gray uniform. He looked young and fresh, not having seen the ugliness of war. She smiled softly. There was a faraway look in Jake's eyes, and Nellie was happy to know that he had been thinking of *her*!

Nellie practically skipped when she left Jake's room that night. She hummed softly as she rounded the bread dough against the hollow of her palm. It wouldn't be long before she would be doing this very same thing in Jake's home! She smiled. He now had a reason to build a kitchen table!

At supper that night, Jake was helped to the table. Although he was feeling stronger in spirits, his leg was still weak. Nellie looked up as he limped into the room. His mouth tightened in a grim line, and he clenched his teeth as he sat down.

When supper was over and the dishes had been washed, she stepped into his room.

"Hey Nellie!" Jake opened his arms as he sat up in bed. Nellie was glad that the open doorway was not in view of their affectionate hug. His bad leg went rigid when she brushed it accidentally.

"I'm sorry!"

Seeing the concern register on her face, he soothed, "It's okay." He smiled warmly. "After this, I really know what Bucky was feeling that day when I pulled him from the trap."

Touching his leg, he muttered, "I felt like I had been clamped in a steel trap, too, when that bullet tore through." He winced, almost as though he felt the shot again. "But Bucky survived, so I can too."

Jake pointed above. "Someone up there was looking after me. Lying in that field, I remembered the scripture your pa read. You know, the one about there being a time for everything." He looked at her intently. "For some reason the Lord didn't take me that day. Guess He knew that I hadn't done everything that verse talked about. You see, I needed a time to love." He smiled, pulling her close, and murmuring in her hair, "Nellie, I love you."

"And I love you," she breathed in a sigh.

A warm feeling spread in her chest. Feeling their hearts beating together, it was almost as if they shared the same organ.

"Nellie"

"Hmm?"

"Read that verse about time when you get a chance. It says a lot."

"Okay," she promised.

Chapter Eighteen

Jake seemed to be feeling better during the next several days, and Nellie was startled to find that he intended to go home before Christmas. Her mother didn't think this was a good idea. She worried that his wound was not healing properly. He had been with them for three weeks now, and the flesh on his leg was still slightly pink.

They were sitting at breakfast, and conversation centered on Jake's upcoming departure.

"But you can't go, Jake. You just got here, " Mary Ann pleaded.

"I'm not leaving right away. You'll see me for a bit longer." He grinned, giving her ponytail a tug.

"Still, I wish you would stay through spring," Martha interjected. "The winter's going to be rough and you shouldn't be alone."

"I appreciate your kindness, Mrs. Morgan, but I'm going to be all right." He looked down, patting his thigh as he spoke.

Nellie thought she detected a slight wince, but he was smiling when he lifted his head.

"Well, if you should change your mind, know that you are always welcome here," her mother said softly.

"Thanks."

Nellie ran her eyes down the muscular length of leg that was stretched beneath the table. Virile and handsome, he had gained back much of his lost weight. The limp had nearly gone from his step. It wouldn't be long before his injury would heal completely. Come spring, they would be working together in the garden.

Later, they sat together near the fire while Rebecca and Laura planned for supper. The girls had insisted on trying a new recipe for dumplings. Martha had smiled, promising to stay out of their way.

Nellie felt the warmth of Jake's hand.

She looked up, meeting his eyes. He looked at her tenderly, tracing a finger along the line of her jaw.

"Nellie."

"Hmm?" she murmured.

"You heard me tell your folks that I'm planning to leave soon." He squeezed her hand gently, lowering his voice. "You've all been good to me, but it's time I took care of myself."

Eyes cast to the floor, she studied the tiny hairline cracks between the planks. Jake didn't have to leave. Didn't he want to be near her?

Laying his hand gently on her slumped shoulders, he spoke softly, "Nell, I don't have to leave alone. You could come with me."

She looked up sharply. Go home with him? What did he mean?

Seeing the puzzled look on her face, he continued softly, "What I'm really trying to say is- you could be my wife. Would you marry me?"

Her breath caught. Had she heard him right? Jake was asking her to be his wife!

"Yes," she whispered, her voice trembling.

Leaning over, he tenderly kissed her cheek.

"I'll ask your pa for his permission tonight."

Following the proposal, she sat numbly, hardly believing that she was going to become Jake's wife, and so soon! Christmas was only a few weeks away!

At supper, Nellie anxiously waited for Jake to speak, barely able to swallow her food.

Hearing Jake clear his throat, she glanced up nervously.

"Joseph and Martha. There's something I'd like to ask of you."

Conversation at the table paused. It was something about his tone that caught everyone's attention.

"Once again, I want to thank you for making me a part of this family. You're some of the most important people in my life, but there's one person here who has become very special to me." He gazed at Nellie tenderly as he spoke. Feeling everyone's eyes, she blushed.

To Joseph, he continued, "Sir, I'd like to ask your permission for Nellie's hand in marriage."

The room was quiet. Nellie held her breath. Her father wouldn't refuse, would he?

"Well, you've been like a son all along, but marriage to Nell will make it official," Joseph answered, wearing a smile.

Martha was at Nellie's side immediately, hugging her daughter close.

"I'm so happy for you, dear."

Chatting excitedly, her sisters were planning the food they'd cook and the dresses they would wear. In a hushed tone, Rebecca reminded them that Nellie was the one getting married, not them. They should be preparing a bridal gown.

"It will be a Christmas wedding!" Martha exclaimed.

Sleep was elusive that night for the girls in the loft. Rebecca quickly slipped under the covers with Nellie.

"Nell, you're so lucky. I hope that someday I marry a man as handsome as Jake," Rebecca sighed.

"And you will. Time will pass so fast that it will surprise you. Why, it seems like yesterday that I was a little girl, younger than you."

"Want to know a secret?" Nellie whispered. Feeling Rebecca's nod, she continued, "Sometimes I *still* feel like a little girl."

Rebecca laughed. "I feel like that sometimes, too. Almost like I am as young as Mary Ann."

They hugged one another and eventually fell asleep, lost in their separate thoughts.

During the next week, the Morgan girls busied themselves with planning the wedding. Nellie and her mother were making a pattern for a bridal gown, and her sisters were making adjustments to their best dresses.

The ceremony would take place on December 24th. It would be the best Christmas Eve ever! In Nellie's excitement, she failed to notice the tired look on Jake's face. It wasn't until the morning that he did not come to breakfast, that she became concerned.

With a worried look in her eyes, Martha left the table. From Jake's room, she heard her mother speaking in soothing tones. Something was wrong! Springing from her chair, Nellie moved quickly into his room.

She stepped back when she saw the pain in Jake's eyes. Martha gestured for her daughter to sit down.

"Jake has been awake for most of the night. Seems like his wound is bothering him again."

Seeing his out-stretched hand, Nellie went to him. As she knelt down by his side, he tried to smile, whispering hoarsely, "Nell, I didn't want you to worry. I haven't said anything because I thought I'd feel better." He gazed at her as he spoke. "It's just that this leg is hurting bad."

"Oh, Jake! Why didn't you tell me?"

"You were having such a happy time. I didn't want to spoil the fun."

"Shhh...now," Martha soothed. Brushing her palm lightly across his brow, she motioned for Nellie to leave.

Getting to her feet, Nellie squeezed Jake's hand tightly. He brought her fingers to his lips, kissing them quickly.

"You go get some breakfast. We don't want both of us sick."

She nodded.

Wearily, she walked into the other room. Noting the sad look on Nellie's face, her family did not ask questions. She went through the motions of eating without tasting the food's flavor. Jake was in pain, and he hadn't told anyone. How long had he been hiding his condition? Guilty, Nellie admonished herself for not spending more time with him during the past week. She should have noticed that he wasn't feeling well.

The clinking of a spoon caught her attention. Her mother stood near the stove, preparing a herbal concoction. This would ease Jake's pain, enabling him to sleep.

Martha spoke softly as she stirred. "Dear, Jake's wound is infected. I suspect that it has been for some time. He just hasn't said anything. With all the excitement, he probably didn't want to dampen our spirits."

"Will he be all right?" Nellie asked.

For a moment, her mother did not speak. She sighed. "I don't know, honey."

Jake would get better. He had to. They were getting married.

The next day Nellie peeped in on him several times, but always found him asleep. Lying on his side, cheek cradled in his elbow, he looked more like a boy than a man.

It was evening when she finally found him awake.

"Hey," he spoke huskily. "Come here."

He held out his arms, a grin in his eyes. Why, he looked so happy!

"You must be feeling better," she murmured, smiling.

"Yeah. It's a bit odd, you know. But I don't feel any pain."

"Really?" she asked, bewildered.

"Guess it has gotten to the point that I can't feel it anyhow. Now it's just gone."

Reaching over, she hugged him tightly.

"While I've been laying here, I've been doing a lot of thinking. Mostly about the war. Wondering if we really knew what we were fighting about. I mean, we thought we were fighting for our land." Shaking his head, he continued, "But from what I've seen, the Yank's dirt looks just the same as ours. And you know, those people we were fighting looked just like you and me."

He sighed deeply, turning to stare at a spot on the wall.

"While I was out there on the ground, there were bodies all around me. Some of them dead, and some of them still breathing. There we were, Rebs and Yanks, all mixed up together. And there was this one boy close by me." He shut his eyes tightly. "Why he was so young! Couldn't have been no more than fourteen. And he was crying. Kept calling for his ma because he knew he wasn't going to make it."

With tears in his eyes, Jake clutched Nellie's hand.

"I was hurting out there, but when I heard that boy cry, it was like I could feel his pain, too. Like it had doubled. It wasn't easy, but I managed to reach him. I held his hand and told him that everything was going to be okay. And you know, he got quiet after a while. So quiet that he didn't speak any more. I could hardly move, but when I turned over, I saw that he was as still as death. That little boy died. And he was a Yank."

Jake wiped a tear from the corner of his eye. He, then, leaned over and kissed the tip of her nose. "And Nellie, I don't want you to worry either, 'cause I'm going to be fine. In fact, I'm so hungry now, I think I could eat a cow!"

"You may feel like that now, but I bet you'd get pretty full just after a few bites!" She kidded with a smile that didn't touch her eyes.

"Well, let's find out," he said. "Go along and tell your ma to set me a place at supper tonight."

Nellie went to give her family the good news. Jake was feeling better!

Supper that night was cheerful, and full of talk. In between the girls' chatter, Joseph discussed readying Jake's cabin for his homecoming. There would be enough firewood to last the winter. Martha would see that they were stocked with canned vegetables from the summer harvest, along with dried apples and potatoes from the root cellar.

Nellie went to bed with a peaceful feeling that night. In her sleep, she felt the same gentle rocking that she had dreamed about since she was small. She was wrapped in a blanket, cradled in her mother's arms. From a distance, she heard singing. The voices washed over her like a lullaby.

We shall meet beyond the river, by and by;
And the darkness will be over, by and by;
There our tears shall all cease flowing, by and by;
All the blest ones, who have gone
To the land of life and song-
We shall meet beyond the river, by and by.

Sounds of movement awakened Nellie the next morning. Her mother and father were speaking in hushed tones, and she caught the trace of worry in her mother's voice.

Curious, she slipped down the ladder, her bare feet hitting the rungs soundlessly.

"Ma, is everything okay?"

The voices fell silent. Her mother backed out of Jake's room, lowering the curtain over the door. She came to stand by her daughter, looking at Nellie with tear-brimmed eyes.

"Nellie," her mother sobbed, "Jake's no longer with us." Wiping her eyes with a cloth, she continued, "The Lord has taken him home".

No! It couldn't be true! No! No! No! He was going to be fine. He had said so himself. Tears burning her eyes, she stared blankly at the wall. She felt her mother reach out, cradling her body. Her chest heaving, Nellie broke away, heading for the door.

Her father reached out to stop her, but Martha intervened.

"No, let her go."

Nellie paid no attention to the frozen ground beneath her bare feet. It was early December, and the weather had taken a turn for the worst. The pain in her chest blocked out the uncomfortable chill that shocked her body.

She could not remember opening the barn door, or climbing behind the rail where her father kept the bundles of hay. Hugging her knees, she rocked back and forth. Sobbing, her chest heaved as she tried to take in air. It wasn't fair! Why did the Lord take him? Didn't He know that they were going to be married in a few weeks?

Closing her eyes tightly, she tried to ward off the agony that wrenched her heart. She wanted to go far away where there were no people, no sounds, and no feelings. Just nothing.

It seemed like only yesterday that they were laughing as they worked together in the field. Once, after she had complained of the heat, he had come up behind her, pouring a mug of water over her head. "To cool you off," he'd teased. She had been furious! And he had smiled, shrugging his shoulders. "Just trying to be helpful," he had added. As if that had made any difference! He had always found a way to justify his silly notions since that first kiss in the woods.

Her lips tingled, remembering the brush of his mouth on her skin. She had been both afraid and excited at the same time! Dark hair had fallen over his sun-bronzed brow, framing his dancing eyes. She shivered, feeling again his warm breath even after he had pulled away.

No! No! No! It couldn't be true. How she grieved for those moments she had taken for granted. There would be no more. Gone. Death and time had taken them away. Never again would she feel the warmth of Jake's presence or hear his husky voice. They wouldn't grow old together and have a family of their own.

She couldn't imagine a tomorrow without Jake in it. Life would be empty. No color. No rich laughter. No silly teasing. Only pain and heartache. There would be no waking up each morning, knowing that their future was another day closer.

And, oh, how could she ever look forward to the coming day? Closing her eyes tightly, she prayed that the Lord would take her, too. She didn't want to live. There was no reason. She would only be a burden to her folks, an old spinster with no where to go.

As a little girl, she had thought that being grown-up was a long time away. But that time had come quickly. Her seventeen years had not taken long. She only hoped that the rest of her life would pass just as quickly. Then it would all be over.

Uncurling her body, she felt the straw scratching her skin. Lifting her head, cold air hit her lungs. Shivering, she hugged her arms to her chest. She breathed deeply, her breath forming a warm cloud. With the cold numbing her body, she gradually rose to her feet.

Making her way to the cabin, she stared at the field lined with trees. The world had not changed with Jake's departure. The sun would still rise and set with each new day. Winter would only last a short while, and spring would bring the earth back to life. Come summer, everything would look pretty again.

The Indians had walked where she stood now, but they were gone. They had left only small reminders of their existence- Cloud Walker's beads, the rock from which the lovers had jumped, and arrowheads nestled where they had last fallen.

The door shut behind her, causing Nellie's parents to look up at her entrance.

"Are you okay, dear?" her mother inquired softly.

She nodded.

Supper that night was quiet. The girls briefly mentioned Christmas, but a sharp look from Joseph cautioned them not to speak. Soon nothing could be heard but the sound of spoons scraping against plates.

Passing Jake's empty room, she felt his absence. Where could he be? Was he looking down at her? Moving by the fire, she picked up her pa's worn leather Bible.

Her loneliness lifted as she turned the pages. She found what she was looking for, almost as though it had been marked. Reading silently, tears rolled down her cheeks.

To everything there is a season, and a time to every
purpose under the heaven: A time to be born, and a

133

time to die; a time to plant, and a time to pluck up that which is planted; A time to kill, and a time to heal; a time to break down, and a time to build up; A time to weep, and a time to laugh; a time to mourn, and a time to dance; A time to cast away stones, and a time to gather stones together; a time to embrace, and a time to refrain from embracing; A time to get, and a time to lose; a time to keep, and a time to cast away; A time to rend, and a time to sew; a time to keep silence, and a time to speak; A time to love, and a time to hate; a time of war, and a time of peace.

Ecclesiastes 3:1

Wiping hot tears from her cheeks, she sobbed softly. *A time to die.* Had that been what Jake was trying to say? No. He wasn't planning to die. There was no thought of death. People didn't die young, only old people. But Jake was gone, and he was never coming back.

What would she do? She didn't know. Nellie handed the marked section to her father.

"This was something Jake asked me to read not long ago. I forgot about it until now."

Joseph peered down at the page, reading the verses aloud. When his voice fell silent, he looked at his daughter with understanding.

"Nellie, one day Rebecca told me about the clock that woke her up every morning. She said you'd explained it to her. Think about that now. You've got a heart in your chest that's still ticking. The good Lord's keeping you here for something. You may not understand just why yet, but everything will work out by and by."

He pulled away, reaching for a folded paper that was lying on the table.

"Nell, I believe there's something Jake meant for you to have."

Opening the coarse parchment, he handed it to his

134

daughter.

"I went though Jake's satchel this morning looking for some way of locating his family. I didn't find anything but a pair of worn moccasins and this."

Not seeing the paper Joseph held in his hand, Nellie gazed at the threadbare toeless moccasins that her father had propped against the satchel heaped on the floor. Tears burning her eyes, she collected the shoes, tracing their outline tenderly. Despite the missing beads, the long-ago Christmas gift was a precious sight!

Nellie held them tenderly while taking the paper, wondering what it might say. The ink scrawling smudged with soil was nearly illegible. She couldn't quite make out the words until she held the writing up to the window's light.

I, Jacob Hunter, being of sound mind and body, knowing that life on Earth is short, desire that upon my death, Nellie Morgan, receive all of my 130 acres and the cabin in which I now live.

In witness of Bill Hunter on this day, April 12, 1862.

Jacob Hunter

Nellie held the worn paper to her breast, tears filling her eyes. She touched the spot where Jake had signed his name. Reading it again, she saw the date- April 12, 1862! That had been her seventeenth birthday! So, he hadn't forgotten.

Carefully, she folded the brittle paper, tucking it inside the Bible. Love was indeed timeless. He, like Cloud Walker, had found a way of keeping close, even in death!

Epilogue

Smoothing back a gray lock of hair, Eleanor leaned more deeply into her chair. Rocking gently before the fire, she turned the photograph face down in her lap. Yes, a lot had happened since that time.

Sixty years ago she hadn't understood why the Lord had taken Jake. She couldn't picture a future without him. But life had continued, and things had changed in a way that she had never expected.

Two years after Jake's death, a church had been built near the mill. Several new families had settled in the region. One of them was a young minister and his two sisters. Having lost their parents to yellow fever, the three had dedicated their lives to the Lord's work. Musically inclined, both girls sang and played a piano they had brought from the east. Near the same age as Rebecca and Laura, the girls had become fast friends.

Eleanor had, unintentionally, felt drawn to their twenty-six year old brother. Down-to-earth in his easy-going manner, he often made her laugh. His smile, along with his coloring and build, were similar reminders of Jake. The resemblance stopped there. Joshua was from a town with cobblestone streets and houses built nearly side by side. Despite their different backgrounds, Nellie had liked Joshua, and she had known that Jake would have too.

At moments, she had been assailed with a sense of guilt, almost as if she was being untrue. But how could she have been unfaithful to a memory? What would Jake have done had she passed away? She knew the answer to that question. He would have found someone else. Maybe he would have married Elizabeth May, after all. But she brushed the thought away for Elizabeth and her mother had moved on. They had returned to their home far away.

Nellie had denied her growing feelings for Joshua until one Sunday morning when he had read the scripture that she could have quoted by heart. Stirring her memory, it was the scripture about time! Nellie had felt as though he was speaking to her alone. His gaze had caused her to look away.

To everything there is a season, and a time to every purpose under the heaven... Indicating the birth of spring and new life, Pastor Joshua had compared people's lives to the changing seasons. Just as the earth endured a loss of greenery in the winter, people, too, suffered losses. A loss took many forms. It could be the death of a loved one, the loss of years to the aged, or the absence of someone who had gone far away.

But the Lord only meant for winter to last a short while. He didn't want his children to mourn forever. Disappointment should not take the place of simple joys. Spring was a time of rebirth and new beginnings, and a person who lived during that season was truly blessed.

Listening to him speak, Nellie had thought about her life. How could things be any different? Jake wasn't coming back, and no one could ever take his place. But her life would go on. She had not died with Jake. What did God have in store for her?

Not long after that particular sermon, Joshua had begun to call. Their friendship had gradually grown into something stronger. It was not long before he had asked her to become his wife, and Nellie had accepted. Yes, she had married the young minister, Joshua Cayton.

Over time, she grew to really care for Josh. Of course, her love for Jake had not diminished, but she and Josh were happy together. The Lord had blessed them with seven children and

137

thirty-eight grandchildren. But someday the Lord would call her home, and there would be someone waiting for her.

"Mammie." The little girl's voice brought Eleanor back to the present. Placing the photograph to the side, she picked up her six- year old great-granddaughter.

"Oh, you're awake, dear."

Cradling her namesake close, she dropped a kiss on Eleanor Abigail's brow.

"Who's that?" Abby asked, pointing to the soldier in the photograph.

Eleanor chuckled. "Oh dear, do you really want to know? Hmm. Where should I begin?"

Leaning back into the rocker, she sighed.

"Let's start with the summer I was fifteen..."

To order autograph copies of *A Time to Love*, complete the information below.

Ship to: (please print)

Name_____

Address_____

City, State, Zip_____

Day Phone_____

_____ copies @ $8.95 each $_____

postage & handing @ $2.95 each $_____

VA residents add .045% sales tax
           ($0.40 each) $_____

                Total amount enclosed $_____

Make checks payable to: Christy L. Hicks
Send to: Once Upon a Lifetime
                1381 Riley Farm Rd.
                Axton, VA 24054